Critical Acclaim f  ks

Miranda and Starlight: *(First of the Starlight series)*

This is an American story of the great outdoors, of following the wisdom of the heart, of wanting love, and living the great American dream. There's magic in the everyday -- "All signs of the early snows had disappeared, the sun shimmered brightly on the dancing leaves of the aspen along the creek." Author Hill writes a spare, sensitive prose and illustrator Lehmkuhl gives us vivid scenes of the girl and the horse. A lovely portrayal of youth and hopes and the high-spirited joy of love. -- ***The Book Reader***

Miranda Stevens is a lonely fifth grader who feels that if she only had a horse of her own everything else in her life would be okay. Then in response to a dare by Chris, a boy who has a habit of bullying others, she mounts a beautiful black horse named Starlight and begins a wonderful adventure of scrapes, narrow escapes, and quandaries that teach Miranda life lessons in honesty, trust, and courage. Beautiful black and white illustrations by Pat Lehmkuhl enhance Janet Muirhead Hill's charming and highly recommended story for young readers.
--Children's Bookwatch

Gr. 4-6. This paperback original is recommended for large collections --and those in horse country. -- ***Carolyn Phelan, Booklist, American Library Association***

Dear Ms. Hill,
I read your book Miranda and Starlight and I really enjoyed it. It was full of life. I felt like I was there watching it all happen. I can't wait to read Starlight's Courage.
-- Jessica Wilson, Age 8"

Starlight's Courage: *(second in the Starlight series)*

Starlight's Courage, by Janet Muirhead Hill, is a must read for any young lady who loves horses. Though it is the second book in the *Starlight* series, *Starlight's Courage* is a great read on it's own. Hill successfully tackles serious issues facing today's youth in a comfortable manner making the book not only entertaining, but also educational.
-- ***Sterling Pearce / GWN Reviewer***

The sequel to *Miranda and Starlight* is the story of a young girl and an injured two-year-old stallion named Starlight that she has befriended. When she and her friends arrange to ride in a competition against their classmates, they are all unaware that a disturbed individual is seeking revenge. An involving and highly recommended novel for young readers. -- ***Midwest Book Review***

Janet Hill writes a rare novel of the upheavals in a young girl's life, capturing the essence of American knowhow. The plotting exerts a sure grip. -- ***The Book Reader***

The intrepid heroine, Miranda, returns in *Starlight's Courage.* Miranda doesn't recognize personal limits—especially when it comes to horses—and this provides Hill with plenty of material for her latest plot. Another easy read for the twelve and under crowd, plus a good choice for parents to read aloud. -- ***Lauren Giannini, In and Around Horse Country***

Preteen girls with equine leanings will certainly enjoy this, rousing sequel, a great stand-alone read, suitable too for discussion group use at the fifth grade level.
-- ***www.thebooxreview.com/featuredchildrensreviews.htm***

Starlight, Star Bright

Janet Muirhead Hill

Illustrated by

Pat Lehmkuhl

Raven Publishing, Norris, Montana

Starlight, Star Bright
by
Janet Muirhead Hill

Published by:
Raven Publishing
PO Box 2885
Norris, Montana 59745
E-mail: Info@ravenpublishing.net

Publisher's note: This novel is a work of fiction. Names, characters, places, and events are either products of the author's imagination or are used fictitiously.

Printed by Banta Book Group, Menasha, WI, USA

ISBN: 0-9714161-2-5
Library of Congress Control Number: 2002095908

Acknowledgements

Many thanks to Buck Brannaman,
author of ***The Faraway Horses,***
for permission to use his name in this book.

Thanks again to my friend and mentor, Florence Ore; to Sharon Beall and her daughter Denise Sarrazin; to Carolyn A. Garber, Zelpha Boyd, and to the creative writing class at Harrison High School; to my sisters Joan Bochmann and Shirley Wertz and to my mother, Dorothy Muirhead; to Jan and Frieda Zimmerman and to all others who have read the manuscript for this book, helped find the mistakes, and offered many worthy suggestions.

To Heather Hickman,

who loved my first two books and said,

"Grandma, you've got to write more."

Chapter One

"Star light, star bright, first star I see tonight." Elliot said as he stared at the evening sky.

Miranda looked down at the little boy beside her. His serious face, sprinkled lightly with freckles across his delicate nose, was lifted toward the sky as he closed his eyes tightly.

"I wish I may, I wish I might, have the wish I wish tonight."

Elliot kept his eyes closed for a long moment after he finished speaking. Miranda kept quiet until he looked up at the sky. Several more stars had come out and a crescent moon was just rising over the distant hills.

"What did you wish for?"

"I can't tell you," he said somberly. "You know it won't come true if I do."

"Who told you that?"

"Mum. We used to sit in the garden every night before bed time and wish on the first star." Elliot's voice cracked and he fell silent.

"What if I already know?" Miranda asked, hoping to take his mind off his loss. His precious "Mum" had died less than a year ago.

"How could you?"

"I just do."

"You don't!" After a pause he added, "But if you do, don't say it. It might jinx it and I want it really bad."

"I won't then, and I hope the stars can make it come true," Miranda said.

She hoped Elliot's wish would come true on his seventh birthday next week. She wondered if she should speak to Elliot's grandfather, Cash Taylor. She wasn't sure if it would help, or if the request would just bring out his stubbornness. She didn't think he liked advice, especially from an eleven-year-old. But, now at least he trusted her to stay with Elliot for a few hours at a time when he had to be away. It made her feel pretty grown up. Mr. Taylor was at a meeting at the school house tonight.

She enjoyed her evening alone with Elliot at the Shady Hills Ranch and Stables. The place had become a second home to her. Starlight, her favorite horse in the world was there and she spent every possible minute with him. Elliot tagged along whenever he could. She didn't mind. He was an interesting child—not only beautiful, but completely honest.

Elliot sighed and continued to stare at the sky as more stars appeared. Miranda took his small hand in hers and said, "Pretty, isn't it. It's fun to see the stars come out, just slowly appearing and getting brighter."

"Do you think Mum is up there somewhere, watching me?" Elliot asked.

"I suppose she is,"Miranda said, though she didn't know what she believed about what became of someone after death. "Maybe my dad is too."

Miranda had never known her father, but missed him, none-the-less. According to Adam, who claimed he knew him in the navy, her dad had died at sea in an attempt to save the life of another sailor. Elliot gripped her hand tighter and they sat in silence. Miranda understood that this would be a very difficult birthday for Elliot and she wondered what she could do to make it easier. She thought of her own birthday two months earlier. She didn't want his to be like that.

Grandma had tried to make it a happy day for Miranda by inviting all the kids from her class over for a surprise party. It had turned out to be awkward and embarrassing. The boys, other than her friend Christopher, hadn't known what to do and clearly didn't like the games Grandma had planned. The girls, except for Laurie, were critical of the old farm house and Miranda's small bedroom.

"You mean you only have one bathroom in your house?" Stephanie had asked. "I have one connected to my room which is about three times the size of yours."

Like Elliot, her greatest wish had been for a horse of her own. She had secretly hoped that Grandpa would buy Starlight from Mr. Taylor. She had dreamed of finding him in their own barn on the morning of her birthday. She had a hard time hiding her disappointment when she opened her gift from her grandparents. It was beautiful: a music box with a black horse inside a glass globe that filled with glittering "snow" when turned upside down. She had swallowed her disappointment and decided, *if I'm ever going to own Starlight I must earn him myself. I won't give up until he's mine.*

Miranda was sure that Elliot longed for a horse; maybe as much as she did. It didn't matter that there were horses available to ride. Having one to call his own was more important than any grownup seemed to understand. She wasn't sure if Elliot had picked out a particular horse, as she had, but she had heard him pouring out his soul to a mare named Sunny one day. He seemed embarrassed when he saw that Miranda had heard, but she understood how comforting it is to talk to a horse about your troubles. Even though horses might not understand the words, they seemed to sense the feelings behind them.

Miranda felt she understood Starlight as much as he understood her. She had nursed him back to health from barbed wire cuts and infection that nearly took his life. In the process, the horse had become as devoted to her as she was to him. Now Starlight was almost three years old, and his only training was what he was learning from her. Most thoroughbreds were running races by his age, but because of his injuries, it had been impossible to start his formal training on schedule.

Higgins, who had been a groom and trainer for Cash Taylor for thirty years, had broken his hip and had to quit working with the horses. He had finally moved back into the bunk house. He wanted to ride again, but so far, all he could do was hobble around with his walker and supervise. Adam Barber, the young man who'd come to Shady Hills to give

Christopher riding lessons, rode and exercised the horses. Good help was hard to find and Adam, who had been hired after Higgins broke his hip, had more to do than he had time for.

"I'll train Starlight," Miranda told Adam when she met him coming out of Starlight's stall yesterday.

"No way!" Adam had shouted. "Don't even think of trying to ride him. You're not a horse trainer. You could ruin him for racing. You've already made such a pet of him, it will be hard to get him groomed for the track. Besides, you can't trust a stallion. He's not a kids' horse so forget that idea!"

It made Miranda angry. If it hadn't been for her, Starlight would be dead. Mr. Taylor had ordered that he be put to sleep when his injuries had left him sick, lame, and scarred. How many times had Mr. Taylor told her that Sir Jet, as he called him, would never be good for anything but a pet? That was until the veterinarian discovered that the tendons and ligaments were not severed. Under his expert care, and with Miranda's help, the horse recovered with not so much as a limp. If you looked closely at his right hind leg, just above the hoof, you could see a wide scar. The one on his left shoulder was barely noticeable.

Adam didn't know that Miranda had been teaching Starlight tricks and voice commands for a long time. The horse responded to her, enjoying the game as much as she did. He came to her call, stopped when she said whoa, followed her around the arena without a lead rope, and even played hide and seek with her. After his injury, Miranda alone had believed in Starlight, now Adam, who was just a hired hand and a new one at that, had the nerve to tell her she didn't know enough to work with him.

Mr. Taylor was late getting home and Elliot was already asleep. Adam, who now lived in the bunk house with Higgins, walked over to stay with the sleeping child while Mr. Taylor took Miranda home.

"Elliot told me his birthday's next week," Miranda said. "Are you going to have a party for him?"

"A party?" Mr. Taylor snorted. "Why would I have a party?"

"Well, because it's his birthday. Everyone expects something special on their birthday."

"I don't. Never had a birthday party in my life. It's foolishness. Getting a year older is a natural part of life. I don't see anything to celebrate."

"Well," Miranda huffed. "Most parents are so glad their kids lived another year that just having their child alive is enough to celebrate!"

"Did Elliot say he wanted a party?"

"No. He didn't say anything about it; in fact he probably doesn't," Miranda conceded.

They drove on in silence for a few moments.

"I suppose I should give him a gift of some kind. What do boys his age like, nowadays?"

"I have some ideas," said Miranda cautiously. "But it depends on how much you were planning on spending."

"Money isn't a problem. You know that. On the other hand, I don't like kids getting spoiled with more toys than they know what to do with."

Miranda thought of the small cardboard box in Elliot's room. Everything in it had been brought from England after his mother died. These were his treasures, but compared to what most kids have, Elliot hardly had any toys.

"I think it should be something he wants very much," Miranda said.

"Do you know what he wants? I sure don't."

"Yes. He wants a horse more than anything in the world."

"A horse? You mean a toy?"

"No, of course not. A real horse. A horse he can ride and take care of and call his very own."

"That's ridiculous! There are over a hundred horses on this ranch. There are at least a dozen that he can ride. Tell me something he doesn't already have!"

"But they're not his horses. And he only gets to ride when a grownup has time to ride with him. You won't let him ride whenever he wants to."

"Of course not. He's not old enough. And that's all the more reason he doesn't need his own horse."

"Well, you asked what he wanted. I was just telling you."

"Well, I think you're wrong. Why would he want a horse when he lives on a horse ranch?"

"If you love a horse, being around him, well, it's hard to explain," Miranda began. "If you live with a horse you love, and you don't know when it will be taken away from you, and you can't take care of it the way your heart tells you is right, it's almost worse than not being around him at all."

"I still don't see what difference it makes whose name is on the registration papers." Mr. Taylor didn't seem to have heard her or have any idea that she was speaking as much for herself as for Elliot. "I don't think it matters to Elliot, at his age."

"That's because it's been so long since you were a little boy. Maybe you forgot how kids feel," Miranda declared, wiping away a tear.

"What makes you think you know what he wants?" Mr. Taylor shouted. "Did he tell you he wants a horse of his own?"

"He doesn't have to tell me. When two people think alike, they just know because they have the same feelings."

"Well, you may think you can read his mind, but I think I know more about boys than you do."

Miranda rolled her eyes in exasperation. She hoped that when she grew up, she wouldn't forget what being a kid was all about.

Grandma was waiting up for Miranda when she entered the kitchen door. She met Miranda with a welcoming hug.

"You have a message from Laurie. She asked

you to call as soon as you got home and said it didn't matter how late it was," Grandma said.

"Is something wrong?" Miranda asked, instantly worried about her best friend.

"Call her and find out," Grandma suggested, handing Miranda the phone. "It did sound rather urgent."

Chapter Two

"Miranda, please come over and spend the night. I have a big surprise for you!" Laurie exclaimed.

"But it's so late. I don't know if I can."

"Ask. I already talked to your Grandma."

"What's the surprise?"

"I want to tell you in person. I promise you'll like it."

"I'll ask," Miranda said, doubtfully.

But Grandma already knew what was coming. Not only did she consent, but she already had Miranda's overnight bag packed.

"I know it's awfully late, Miranda," Mrs. Langley said when she arrived. "My husband has a week off from work. He called on his way home yesterday and asked us where we'd like to go for a short vacation. Laurie came up with a grand idea, and we just got the details worked out today."

"What is it?" Miranda asked excitedly.

"It's a trail ride up in the mountains. You know, a pack trip, like the girls at school are always bragging about," Laurie answered.

"You mean horses? Where will we get the horses? Who all is going? I don't have my camping gear!" Miranda hopped up and down in excitement.

Mrs. Langley laughed. "Yes you do," she said. "Your grandmother put your sleeping bag inside the porch before she left."

"The best part is the horses, Miranda. I couldn't believe it when I got up this morning and got my birthday present."

"Your birthday isn't until August," said Miranda. "This is June."

"I know. Mom and Dad decided to give it to me early when we decided to do this. Here Miranda, look at this," Laurie exclaimed, putting a piece of paper in Miranda's hand.

"It's from the Montana Thoroughbred Association. Laurie, you got a horse for your birthday! I can't believe it! Oh, my gosh! It's Lady. You're the one who bought Lady?" Miranda exclaimed as she saw the name "Grand Cadillac's Ladyslipper" on the paper.

"Mom and Dad did about four or five months ago, but they were saving it for my birthday."

"Well, that explains it! I wondered who Mr. Taylor sold her to and why the owners didn't come get her. I love that horse. Elliot and I both wanted to ride her, but Mr. Taylor wouldn't let us. He said she belonged to someone else and put her out in the field. I saw her from the school playground, sometimes."

"Yeah, me too. But I had no idea she was mine. Isn't she the one you rode the first day of school? I was so scared when I watched you get on her, and then Starlight started chasing her. I was sure you would be killed. I watched you all the way across the field. I was so relieved when I saw you get stopped and get off safely."

"That seems so long ago, but it hasn't even been a year. But, Laurie, what about the trail ride? You'll ride Lady, but..."

"Oh, don't worry. We borrowed Queen for you to ride, and Mom and Dad rented horses from Mr. Taylor, one for each of them to ride and two pack horses. Adam is going to haul them up to the trail head in one of Mr. Taylor's trailers."

"Chris didn't mind loaning Queen?"

"Not when he heard you'd be riding her," Laurie answered with a teasing smile.

"Enough talk, girls. It's almost eleven. Your father's been asleep for over an hour, Laurie. He'll be up and ready to hit the trail while you two are still snoozing. Please go right to sleep."

"It's nice your dad is home," Miranda said as they crawled into bed. "I'll finally get a chance to meet him."

Meeting Mr. Langley was a surprise. He was tall and thin with smooth skin the color of a milk chocolate candy bar. His dark eyes were his most impressive feature. They were clear and kind and sparkled with good humor. His crew cut hair was black and thick. Miranda could see where Laurie got her long, curling eye-lashes and straight nose. They were just like her father's, though her round face and dimpled cheeks were more like the sweet face of her blonde, blue-eyed mother. Laurie giggled when her father came out of his room the next morning.

"Dad, where did you get those clothes?"

"I went shopping in Spokane on my way home. I own nothing but slacks, suits, and sports coats," he said, turning around like a fashion model. "I had to look the part if I was going to be a cowboy, didn't I?"

His shirt was a shiny sky blue, but the long scalloped sleeve cuffs and the yoke across the shoulders were bright silver. He wore new blue jeans and cowboy boots with fancy red stitching. His belt buckle was the biggest Miranda had ever seen, shiny silver and gold. He looked like something out of one of the old Roy Rogers movies Grandpa had shown her.

"Uh, Dad, people around here wear their pants over their boots, not tucked in," Laurie said.

Adam helped them put their camping gear into the panniers on the pack horses. When the other horses were saddled and ready, Adam told them good-bye and promised to be back Sunday afternoon to pick them up. It was Friday morning.

Miranda was happy to be riding Queen, Christopher Bergman's tall sorrel mare. The scenery was beautiful and the air brisk and cool. All of the horses were frisky and eager to start.

"Whoa! Help!" cried Mrs. Langley, as Cinder, the bay gelding she was riding, sprang into a gallop to get ahead of Lady and Queen.

Miranda looked around to see Mrs. Langley's hat fly off of her blonde hair as she bounced along holding onto the saddle horn with both hands.

"Pull back on the reins, Mom!" Laurie yelled.

"Hang on, Honey!" called Mr. Langley as he caught her hat.

"I'm okay. Whew!" gasped Mrs. Langley.

Her horse slowed to a walk, as if nothing had happened. He was out in front, now, and content to set a slow pace.

"It's been a while since I rode, and I was taken by surprise, but don't worry about me," Mrs. Langley said, taking her hat from her husband.

After climbing a series of switchbacks, they rode through a grove of quaking aspen as the trail straightened and slowly climbed. Miranda loved the fluttering pale green leaves. She scanned the white branches for birds' nests. Scattered on the forest floor beneath the green canopy were bright yellow glacier lilies. Miranda, entranced with the beauty, dreamed she was a tiny fairy, flitting from flower to flower and soaring up into the trees to look into the bird nests. She would find one with baby birds in it and ask if she could sleep with them when the night got cold.

"Oh, would you look at that!" exclaimed Mrs. Langley.

Miranda was brought back to earth when Queen stopped short, nearly bumping into Cinder. Nudging Queen to move up beside him, she gasped at the beautiful view of the valley below.

"Wow! You can see forever from up here. Look at that little lake over there. And there's another one," she said, pointing.

"They look like little mirrors. Maybe some giants use them when they shave in the morning," said Laurie. "And look at that flat-top mountain. That must be his table, and that round hill is his stool."

"What an imagination!" exclaimed her mother.

"I can see it! And there's the giant sleeping," said Miranda, pointing to a mountain ridge. "See? That first hump is his head, then his chest, and he has his knees up. Over there is his big toe sticking up."

"No wonder you two get along so well," said Mrs. Langley.

The trail steepened and the rocky slope on their left crowded the trail dangerously close to a sheer drop off that ended in a raging mountain stream far below.

"No one told me about this," Mr. Langley said nervously as the horses plodded single file, seemingly unworried. "Don't look down."

Of course Miranda did. She was thrilled at the sight of the rushing water, the rainbow that hovered above it, and the bed of wild flowers on the other side.

"Look! A moose!" she shouted.

A bull with huge spooned antlers stood in the middle of the stream where a log jam created a quiet pool. At this point, the trail widened again, and a few feet of grass and shrubbery separated them from the steep drop off. They stopped to watch the ungainly creature below as he dipped his head into the knee deep water.

At noon, they rested near a waterfall as they ate their lunch and let the horses graze. They had watered the horses about a half-mile back, where the clear mountain stream crossed the trail. The peanut butter sandwiches they'd fixed that morning were delicious. Funny how the mountain air could make such ordinary food taste so good. This was the life she was made for, Miranda decided.

"When we get our horse ranch, Laurie, we'll make sure it's in the mountains. We can go on pack trips every weekend!"

"What's this about a horse ranch?"asked Mr. Langley.

"Miranda and I are going to have a ranch together when we grow up. Starlight is going to be our stallion and we'll have Lady and get a lot of other mares and raise race horses..." Laurie began.

"Only trouble is," Miranda interrupted, "Starlight isn't mine. I think I'm the only kid in my class who doesn't have a horse."

Miranda was ashamed as soon as the words left her mouth. She didn't want to spoil the day by whining, but it just slipped out.

"I'm sure you will, one day, Miranda." Laurie said. "Mr. Taylor might decide to pay you for all the work you do around there. He should give you Starlight instead of money."

"Not likely. I thought I could talk him into it when Starlight was lame, but now they're talking about racing him. Mr. Taylor told Adam to start his training. If Starlight wins a race, Mr. Taylor will never sell him to me."

"Perhaps you can buy another horse from him,

or from someone else," Mr. Langley suggested. "I know some people over by Willow Creek who have some nice saddle horses for sale."

"I don't want any horse but Starlight."

Miranda knew she sounded ungrateful when Mr. Langley was trying to cheer her up, but she couldn't help it. Since the first day she laid eyes on Starlight, she had dreamed of owning him. She didn't think she could ever love any other horse as much as she loved him.

With the beauty all around her Miranda quickly forgot about feeling sorry for herself. She and Laurie tried to see who could spot the most wild animals. There were chipmunks, marmots, and deer. Laurie saw a sleepy owl in a tree, and Miranda spotted a pair of golden eagles circling overhead. By the time they reached Bell Lake, which was their destination, the sun was hanging low over the nearby peaks.

"Oh, ouch! I don't think I'll ever be able to walk, sit or ride again," cried Mrs. Langley as she dismounted.

"I know what you mean," said her husband. "Why didn't we take a few short rides before we attempted an all day trek up the mountains on these four legged torture seats."

"I'm not sore," bragged Miranda. "Are you, Laurie?"

"Nope! I feel great," Laurie agreed with a teasing laugh.

Mr. Langley unloaded the pack horses, while Miranda and Laurie unsaddled and brushed out the others. They put halters on them and tied them all to a long picket line which Miranda tied to a tree in the middle of a grassy clearing. Mrs. Langley organized the food and began setting up the two tents.

"I'll make a table out of logs for our kitchen," offered Mr. Langley. "There's a tarp to put over it. I'll get that hung, too.

"We'll gather some fire wood," offered Miranda.

She and Laurie ran off into the woods. By the time they had dragged in a lot of dead fall and piled it beside the ring of rocks left by the campers before them, Mr. Langley had a fire blazing, and Mrs. Langley was frying hamburgers and heating up some beans. It tasted so good that Miranda didn't think she'd ever get enough, but before long she was so full she didn't want to move. She yawned. It was contagious, for soon everyone around the campfire was yawning too.

"You girls rinse out your dishes in that pan of water and then go to bed. It's been a long day. We'll put the food away and hit the sack ourselves," said Mrs. Langley.

After crawling into the small tent with Laurie, Miranda listened to Mr. and Mrs. Langley discussing the merits of hoisting the food, now wrapped and back in the panniers, high off the ground.

"I'm so tired. Are you sure we need to hang it

from a tree branch?" Mrs. Langley asked.

"This is bear country, dear, I think we should take all the recommended precautions."

But Miranda heard no more as she snuggled into her warm sleeping bag and drifted into dreamland.

Miranda jumped as a loud noise interrupted her dream. She sat up and rubbed her eyes.

"Did you hear that?" Laurie whispered.

"Sounded like someone dropped something metal. Listen!" Miranda said as the horses snorted and stomped.

Both girls crawled to the tent flap at once, bumping heads in the dark.

"Stay where you are, girls, and keep quiet," ordered Mr. Langley in a stage whisper.

Peering from the door of the tent, Miranda saw a black bear in the beam of Mr. Langley's flash light. It batted the empty coffee pot across the ground. Frozen in fascination, she stared as the bear licked the ground where the grease from the hamburgers had been poured. Finding no other food, the bear lumbered toward the girls' tent.

Chapter Three

"Where's my bell? The bear bell!" shouted Mr. Langley, as the flashlight disappeared into the Langley's tent, leaving the bear in darkness.

Miranda held her breath, listening, as she tried to make out the bear's dark form. Just as her eyes began to adjust to the darkness, the flashlight came on and beamed on the bear again. It hadn't moved. Blinking, it turned away and sauntered back toward the coffee pot. Preston Langley's bell began clanging. The bear stopped, looked back, and then trotted up the hill and out of sight. The horses calmed down immediately, but the girls ran to the Langley's tent. They couldn't stop talking about what they had just seen.

"It's a good thing I read up about camping in bear country," Mr. Langley said.

"I thought your bell was pretty stupid, but I

guess I was wrong. At least I didn't have to use my pepper spray. I hope I never get that close," Mrs. Langley said.

"I never took a bell or pepper spray on a camping trip before. I thought just city slickers did that," Miranda said, then added with embarrassment, "No offense!"

"I'd rather be a city slicker, scaring a bear away with a bell than a macho mountain man inside of one," said Mr. Langley with a chuckle.

"It sure was cute, though, wasn't it. I'm glad it decided to go away," added Laurie.

"Yeah, me too, but I don't think he would have hurt us. It was a black bear, not a grizzly. I think it was just curious," Miranda said.

"Well, I guess it's a good thing I hoisted the food bags into the tree last night, or it might have been around a lot longer, and we might have been without breakfast," said Mr. Langley.

Miranda looked up as Mr. Langley shined his flashlight into a nearby tree. She saw the panniers hanging from a tall branch. She also noticed that the eastern horizon was turning rosy.

"Well, I'm going back to bed," Mrs. Langley said. Miranda and Laurie went back to their tent.

They talked for several minutes, until Laurie's voice trailed off sleepily in the middle of a sentence. Miranda felt wide awake, but closed her eyes. The sound of birds twittering, fire crackling, and a horse cropping grass just outside her tent soothed her into a peaceful doze. Then she smelled smoke. She sat up and glanced at the sleeping bag next to hers. Laurie was sleeping soundly.

She peeked out the tent flap to see Mr. Langley stooping over the fire to place more wood in a teepee formation over the small flames. She studied him carefully. He was wearing the same blue shirt, but the sleeves were rolled up and he'd left off his belt. She noticed he was wearing a pair of old slippers as he puttered around the fire. He stopped every few minutes to look around him with an expression of pleasure. There was something about his face that was comforting. He looked both wise and kind, Miranda decided; someone she could trust. *How could anyone not like him?* she wondered.

Miranda had learned through the meanness of four of her classmates, that Laurie was part African American. They actually called her a nigger! Both her mother and her grandparents had made it clear to Miranda that "nigger" was a demeaning word; disrespectful and insulting, and she must never use it. Though she had never known a black person intimately, she'd seen many in California, and they seemed to be treated just like everyone else. She felt angry and confused by her classmates attacks of Laurie's family. What difference did it make where your ancestors came from? Laurie was, in Miranda's eyes, the most beautiful girl she'd ever seen, with her deep brown eyes, long brown curls and a dimple in each cheek. Miranda loved her.

The animosity between Miranda and her friends and their classmates had finally become a rather indifferent and sometimes tense sort of truce. Mr. Langley was a bit of a curiosity to Miranda, not because of the color of his skin, but because he seemed so different in other ways from the men she knew in the community.

"Good morning. You're up early," called Mr. Langley as Miranda stepped out of the tent into the cool mountain air. "You couldn't sleep either, eh?"

"I'm used to getting up early. Besides there is so much to see and do up here, I didn't want to miss any of it," Miranda answered, crouching by the fire.

"I'm in the habit of getting up early, too. I have

to when I'm working. But that bear had my adrenalin pumping like crazy. Not much chance of sleeping after that," Mr. Langley said, shaking his head.

"I thought he was so cute. I've seen bears before and they don't really scare me, but I love seeing them," Miranda bragged.

"Really? You weren't even a little bit scared when he was marching right toward your tent?"

"Well, yeah, I guess I was; but just for a minute."

"Where have you seen bears before?"

"Grandpa lost a few calves last summer to a contagious disease calves get sometimes. Well, he buried the dead ones out in the edge of the pasture by the trees, but something kept digging them up and dragging them off. We thought it was dogs at first, but Grandpa let me stay up with him one night and watch. It was bears."

"Well, I have to admit, this is the first time I've seen one that wasn't behind bars, and I was scared half to death. Now that it's over, though, I'm glad I got to see it," Mr. Langley said.

"Behind bars? I hate that! I went to a zoo in California one time. The animals didn't look happy. I just wanted to let them all loose."

"Now that could have been a disaster for both the people and the animals. But I know what you mean. Being out in nature like this gives a person a sense of freedom you don't get in the city. As I listened to the mountains come alive this morning I knew I didn't want to waste a minute of this vacation. I always dreamed of getting away into the mountains, but this is a first-time experience for me."

"Really?" Miranda was surprised. "You sure seem to know what you're doing."

"Oh, I've camped before. I was a Boy Scout for many years. But I grew up in Cincinnati, and the camping we did was never in such a lofty setting."

"What was it like, growing up in an eastern city?" Miranda asked. "I lived close to Los Angeles for awhile and I didn't like it much. I'd rather live in the country."

"City life is different in a lot of ways, but there are good and bad things about it, just like here," Mr. Langley said. "Life is what you make it, no matter where you are."

"What do you mean? I like wide open spaces with lots of animals and not many people. You can't get that in a city," Miranda argued.

"No, you can't find this kind of beauty, but you can find beauty and goodness in the people and places that are there."

"So, people were always nice to you in Cincinnati?"

Mr. Langley laughed softly. "Did I say that? No, you can find meanness, too, wherever you go. It's no different here. What's important is whether you let the beauty or the meanness become a part of you."

When Mrs. Langley and Laurie stumbled from their tents, hot chocolate and coffee were ready for them. Mr. Langley cooked breakfast as they sipped their beverages and slowly came alive. Miranda moved the horses to fresh grass, retying their picket line.

After breakfast, they saddled the horses and headed up the trail for the top of the ridge. The higher they climbed, the thinner and shorter the trees were until only low shrubbery could be seen. The air was thin, crisp, and cool, and the view was sharp and clear for many miles. They came upon large patches of snow, yet many kinds of flowers in yellow, purple, and blue stood among the lichens and short grass.

It was noon when they finally reached the top of the ridge. They could see the trail winding down the other side and more mountain lakes scattered below. They dismounted and ate their lunches quietly. Everyone seemed to be in awe of the beauty that surrounded them, as each reveled in his or her private thoughts.

"Can we ride down to that lake?" Laurie broke the silence as she pointed.

"That's a lot farther than it looks. I read that sign over there and the nearest lake in that direction is seven miles," her father told her.

"It took us half a day to get here, so I suppose we'd better get started back soon," added Mrs. Langley.

"May we climb those rocks over there, first?" Miranda asked. "It won't take long."

"Sure. We'll sit here and watch. I'll give you a

half hour to explore," Mr. Langley told them.

The girls ran to a rocky outcropping near the summit of the nearest peak. As they scrambled over the rocks, a marmot ducked into a crevice. A chipmunk chattered at them, and a raven glided overhead, issuing one loud croak before swooping down the other side of the mountain.

"If we hurry we can climb to the very top," Miranda suggested.

"Let's do. It would be a shame to be this close and not stand on the very highest point," Laurie agreed, so the girls ran up the gentle incline.

"Look! What's that?" Laurie asked.

"Goats," Miranda declared. "They're just babies."

Two little mountain goats, as white as the snow, scampered across the steep shale slopes below them.

"How cute!" Laurie exclaimed.

"Look how they run and jump across those rocks like it was nothing. How do they stick when it's so steep? You'd think for sure they'd fall to the bottom," Miranda observed in amazement.

Soon they stood on the very top of the mountain. Looking in every direction, Miranda felt a sense of excitement and happiness she had never known before. The view in every direction made the world look small, as if she were somehow bigger than all of it. Yet it stretched out for miles and miles of endless nature. Not a living person or sign of civilization could be detected. *There's nothing like this, yet it's always been here. I must come back again,* she thought.

When the weary riders arrived back at their camp, Miranda volunteered to take charge of the horses while the others gathered wood and cooked supper. (The Langley's called it dinner, but by what ever name, it was warm, tasty, and satisfying.) After dark, they told stories around the campfire until Miranda nearly fell off the log she was sitting on as she nodded off.

"Okay, time for bed everyone. We'll have to get up early to break camp. Adam said he'd meet us at three thirty," Mr. Langley said. The girls didn't argue and were soon snug in their sleeping bags.

"Laurie, I had so much fun today. Your mom and dad are really nice. I'm glad you invited me," Miranda whispered.

"Me too!" Laurie said.

"How did your dad learn to ride?"

"Mom got him to take riding lessons at a stable near Cincinnati, where I learned to ride. Mom grew up with horses, but Dad had never even seen one until he met Mom."

"Are you serious?" Miranda was amazed to think that anyone could grow up without even seeing a horse.

"He never had a chance. His mom made sure he kept busy. She didn't want him to get into a gang like some of the other kids. She always told him he was going to go to college. So he found after school jobs and worked hard and saved money. Grandma and Grandpa Langley helped him all they could and he went to college and met Mom. He taught school for awhile, and after Mom got him interested in horses, he hooked up with a farm and ranch supply company because they offered him more money."

"And he likes that better?"

"No, he wants to teach. He thought he was going to be the math teacher at the school here. They told him he had the job, but when we got here and they saw he was black, they made up excuses. They said there had been a misunderstanding. So he went back to selling."

Miranda lay awake a long time, seething at the injustice of what she'd just heard. Only after she turned her thoughts to the beauties she had seen that day did she fall asleep. She dreamed of flying like the raven that had visited them on the mountain top. Suddenly a horse squealed and she dreamed she was riding Starlight across an alpine meadow. His thundering hooves echoed and he snorted loudly. Miranda turned over and went on dreaming.

"Miranda! Where are the horses?"

Miranda sat up with a start. It was no longer dark. She rubbed her eyes, not quite sure if she'd actually heard Mr. Langley call her name or if it was part of her dream. Peering out of the tent, she saw him standing near the empty fire ring, turning in circles as he looked about. She looked to the picket line for the horses. There was not a horse in sight.

Chapter Four

Miranda stumbled out of the tent in her flannel pajamas. She ran in every direction looking for the horses and calling each one by name. She whistled.

"Miranda, I think they're long gone," Mr. Langley said. "Your feet are going to freeze. You'd better get dressed."

"I was sure I tied them well. Their halter ropes were already tied to the picket line. All I did was hook them to the halters. It held the night before so I thought..."

"It's okay, Miranda. No one is blaming you," Mr. Langley said. "Look! The rope is gone from the tree, but here are some pieces of it. It looks like something chewed it apart."

Miranda stared up into the tree.

"Oh, look. See how the bark is eaten in places. Porcupines do that. And it looks fresh."

"Well, look at that! You're right. There it is."

Miranda hurried to Mr. Langley's side and stared up higher and higher until she saw a furry black ball on a branch. As she watched, it blinked once, and then beady black eyes stared down at them.

They tried to track the horses, but it was hard to tell yesterday's tracks from todays. There were places where the dusty earth and pine needles had been smoothed as if swept with a broom.

"They're dragging the picket line," Mr. Langley said. "They are probably still all tied together."

"Let's follow that track!" Miranda said excitedly.

It seemed to follow the trail, but soon disappeared on the rocky surface.

"Well, there is only one thing we can do. It's obvious the horses headed down the trail the way we came. We'll eat breakfast and then clean up camp. We can pack everything in the panniers."

"But the horses are just getting farther away," Miranda protested.

"There isn't much hope of us catching up with them. They may have been gone half the night," Mr. Langley reasoned. "We'll have to start walking. If we don't find the horses before we get back, we'll meet Adam as planned and then get some help searching for them."

"I can't go back without Queen! Chris will kill me if anything bad happens to her!" Miranda declared. "And what will Mr. Taylor say? He'll be furious. He might sue us!"

"I don't know what else to do," Mr. Langley said. "And don't worry so much!"

Miranda ate hurriedly and began taking down the tent and putting packs and sleeping bags near the panniers for Mr. and Mrs. Langley to pack. At last they were ready to go. Even though the trail was mostly downhill, it seemed to take forever. Once in a while they'd pick up horse prints in the dusty trail or in the mud where a small stream crossed the trail. Miranda wanted to run, but Laurie's parents insisted that they all stay together. By one o'clock, they still hadn't reached the waterfall where they had lunched on the way up. Mrs. Langley's feet were hurting, so they stopped at a small foot bridge where the path crossed the stream. As they ate their lunch, Mrs. Langley soaked her feet in the cold water. She had several blisters where her boots rubbed.

"Your boots must be too big," her husband said. "I have an extra pair of socks. Put them on and see if it helps."

"May we please go on ahead," Laurie pleaded. "We'll stay on the trail."

"No. You could get lost or fall into the gorge below the waterfall, or get eaten by a bear or..."

"We'll be careful, and if we make noise, it'll just scare any bears away. There aren't any grizzlies in these mountains," Miranda pleaded.

"Please, just stay with us. We're almost ready."

Mrs. Langley pulled her boots on with a groan

and stood up.

"That feels better. I can't believe I started out without grabbing the first aid kit. I know exactly where it is in the panniers," she said.

"Here, I'll carry you piggyback," Mr. Langley offered when his wife began limping again.

She accepted the offer and they picked up the pace for awhile.

"Look, there's a mile marker," Miranda said, glancing at her watch. "Oh dear, three miles to go and it's almost four o'clock."

"Hello, there. Glad to see you're all okay!" a voice called, as if in answer to her worry. "I found these nags waiting at the parking area."

It was Adam riding Cinder bareback and leading the other five horses, still on their picket line. For once, Miranda was glad to see him.

Miranda talked the whole way to Shady Hills, Monday afternoon, telling Chris all about their camping trip.

"What a relief it was to see Adam with all the horses. I had visions of having to tell you your horse was lost."

"What did you do after you met Adam?" Chris asked.

"Laurie's mom chose to wait, but the rest of us rode bareback all the way back to the camp so we could get the saddles and packs. It was after dark when we got back to Mrs. Langley and she sure was

glad to see us. It was past midnight when we got home and Grandma and Grandpa were worried."

"No wonder you slept in this morning," Chris said as they got out of the Bergman's mini-van at Shady Hills.

"I can't stay long today. I'm entertaining the garden club at my house and I have a lot to do to get ready," Chris's mother informed them as they came to a stop in front of the stables.

It had been Grandma's idea to take turns with Laurie's and Chris's mothers to take the kids to the stables and stay with them while they rode. Miranda had never liked the idea. She didn't think they needed supervision, but the concussion she got from falling off a horse one day was enough to convince her grandmother that they did.

"You know, I bet it would be all right if you

didn't stay with us today," Miranda said. "Adam is working and Higgins is always in the bunk house. Mr. Taylor's probably home, too, so we'll have plenty of grownups around if we have any trouble."

"Well, that's true," Mrs. Bergman said. "I guess it would be all right. Just promise you'll wear your helmets while you ride."

The helmets were also an idea of Grandma's that Miranda hated even worse than the other. The lightweight riding helmet that her Grandma tried to tell her was stylish was totally dorky in Miranda's opinion. She didn't like having anything on her head; she preferred letting the wind blow through her hair.

Chris promised his mother that they would wear their helmets, and she gladly left them to fend for themselves as she hurried off to do her own things.

Miranda ran to Starlight's stall first thing. He was out in his paddock, cropping the short grass with his sharp teeth. His black coat glistened in the bright sunshine and his muscles rippled when he moved. He had filled out a lot and was very nearly full grown. *How tall and majestic he is,* thought Miranda. *He should be running races. I bet he could beat anyone.* Remembering when she had been on his back for a few brief minutes; the power of his muscles beneath her and the wind in her face, she desperately wanted to ride him again.

"Hi, half-pint!" called a cheerful voice from the stable door. "How would you like to muck out this stall for me."

It was Adam Barber. When Adam first came to Shady Hills to give Chris riding lessons, he had been cold and rude to Miranda. Now he was often friendly, but Miranda was never sure what to expect from him.

"Why are you cleaning stalls? I thought Mr. Taylor had hired a man for that job."

Miranda decided to ignore that he'd called her half-pint. She guessed it was because he had been friends with her father in the navy that he thought he had the right to tease and belittle her. He'd acted that way since he told her about the tragic accident that swept her father into the sea, never to be seen again.

"He never showed up today," Adam answered. "Got paid last night and probably skipped town. That seems to be our luck around here."

"I'll take care of Starlight. You know I always do unless someone beats me to it."

"Thanks. I have the rest of them done. Mr. Taylor's waiting on me to go with him to look at some horses up north of Helena."

Miranda smiled to herself as she forked the dirty shavings into a wheel barrow. She soon had the stall clean and the water trough filled. Seeing no one around, she went to the tack shed and found a bright red halter that looked great on Starlight. She also took a bridle and an English saddle to Starlight's stall. Starlight saw her coming and trotted up the paddock to meet her. He nuzzled her shirt pockets. Laughing she gave him the sugar cube she had brought for him, slipped the halter on him and led him to his stall.

"What are you doing?" Chris asked from the doorway.

"Chris! You are always sneaking up on me."

"I am not! You just don't notice anything except what you're thinking about. Are you trying to put a saddle on him?"

"You have to keep a secret, Chris. It's a surprise. I've been working with him from the ground quite a bit and I thought this would be a good time to get him used to the saddle. Somebody has to train him. Higgins can't and Adam never has time."

"So, I take it you don't think we should call our parents and tell them there are no grownups here to watch over us." Chris teased.

"Higgins is here. I'm just hoping he stays in his house."

"Wrong. His nephew just came and took him to a doctor's appointment. See? Like I said; you don't notice anything but what you're concentrating on."

"Chris this is perfect! Just promise not to tell and we can work with Starlight all day. He doesn't seem at all afraid of the saddle. I bet he'll let me put it on him."

Miranda had been rubbing Starlight's withers with the stirrup. Starlight liked it. Now she placed the saddle against his side and slowly moved it up until it rested on his back. Again, she used the stirrup to caress his side. Scratching his chest with her finger nails she slowly pulled the girth around him and loosely buckled the billet strap. He seemed to consider it all part of a luxurious massage.

"Wow, you did it!" Chris shouted.

Starlight jumped sideways at the sudden loud voice. The saddle slipped and swung beneath him. Frightened by the unfamiliar sensation, he bucked and kicked. All Miranda could do was stand out of the way and beg him to calm down. When he finally stopped jumping around, he was trembling.

"Chris. Please quit your bellowing? You're always startling people, horses included."

"Sorry," Chris said softly, "I won't say another word."

Miranda spoke in a soft voice and went to Starlight's head. She offered him another sugar cube and patted his nose. As he gradually calmed down, she went to his right side. Standing on tiptoes, she could barely reach the buckle. It took her awhile to get it undone, but her voice continued to soothe the stallion and he didn't move. Then she started all over. He was more suspicious of the saddle this time but she gradually won his confidence and soon had it in place. This time she snugged the girth a little tighter. He didn't seem to mind.

"Let's take him to the round pen. It's smaller than the arena," Miranda said, opening the stable door.

Chris followed and Miranda led Starlight around the corral, first one way and then the other.

He never seemed to notice the saddle.

"It's almost lunch time," Chris said finally. "It's such a nice day, let's both get on Queen and go to the pasture to eat our lunches."

"I have a better idea. You take Queen and I'll take Starlight."

"You can't ride him!"

"I bet I could, but I didn't say I was going to, not out in the open yet. But I can lead him. It'll give him a chance to get used to the saddle. I'll tie the bridle to it so he has something slapping against his shoulder. I'm trying to get him used to things gradually so he won't spook so easily."

"I'll get Queen saddled and get our lunches," Chris offered.

Miranda took Starlight back to his stall, tied the bridle to his saddle and then scratched his left shoulder with the bit. As Miranda led him down the paddock and back, he didn't seem to notice the saddle on his back. Maybe he's ready for more, she thought. She stopped him beside the tall white board fence that divided his paddock from another. As she petted and scratched his neck, she scooted up the rails backward, until she was even with his tall back. Still talking to him, she put her right leg over his back and eased into the saddle, most of her weight still resting on her left foot on the fence. He flipped an ear back quizzically and turned his head to look at her. She lowered herself gradually until all of her weight was in the saddle.

Chapter Five

Her heart pounded as she realized what she had done. She was so excited that she wanted to shout, "Look at me. I'm on Starlight!" but she only whispered, "Thanks"and stepped onto the fence again.

"Miranda, I saw that!" Chris called from the stable door. "And I didn't even say anything."

Miranda was glad that he saw. She felt like she had just done something wonderful and she didn't want it to go unnoticed. But she made him swear not to tell. No one else must know what she was doing until she and Starlight were ready. For now, it was a secret shared only with Christopher Bergman.

"Are you ready to go eat? I'm getting hungry," Chris complained.

"I guess so. Do you suppose I could ride him?"

"Not in the pasture. You don't know what he might do. You may ride with me if you want."

"Well, maybe to start with. I'll get on behind you and lead Starlight. Let's go up in the hill pasture."

"I thought the river pasture was your favorite," Chris said. "It's prettier and has more shade."

"The hill pasture is more open. Not so many hazards. I think the river might scare him."

Miranda remembered how Starlight had shied at a stream and ended up in a bog that nearly took his life on that fateful day that had changed both their lives. Not that it would happen again, but the hill pasture seemed less threatening.

Miranda led Starlight through the pasture gate and then closed it after Chris rode Queen through. She let Chris hold Starlight's halter rope while she got on Queen behind Chris's saddle. He was riding English, so there wasn't much for her to hold on to. Not that she needed to hold on, she told herself. Starlight's ears were pricked forward as he looked around at the wide open space.

Chris cued Queen with his knees and Miranda tugged Starlight's rope as they started forward. Starlight, resisted for a moment, nearly pulling Miranda off. Then he swung in behind, lay back his ears and nipped Queen's rear end. The mare leaped forward into a gallop.

"What the heck?!" Chris shouted, grabbing the pommel of his saddle.

Miranda felt herself slipping and grabbed Chris around the waist. Starlight lowered his head and

nipped at Queen's heels, jerking the rope from Miranda's hand. Queen sped forward, running full out up a sagebrush covered hill.

"We have to stop her," Miranda shouted. "Chris, let go of the saddle and pull back on the reins."

She reached for the reins, but Chris already had them in his hands and was pulling back. Queen tried to stop, but the stallion bit her rump and she took off again.

"Stop it! Starlight, quit!" she yelled waving one free hand at him as she bounced behind the saddle.

The stallion veered away and Queen slowed again.

"Jump off, quick," Miranda ordered.

As Queen came to a bumpy stop, they half fell and half jumped from the saddle.

"I got our lunches," Chris said stupidly, holding a burlap bag as he sat up on the ground.

Miranda stared, digesting this insane comment. Chris looked surprised as he stared at the bag. Suddenly Miranda laughed. She was stunned, excited, scared, and felt like crying, but the silliness of the situation and relief that neither of them was hurt made her laugh until her sides hurt. Chris looked at her as if she were crazy and then chuckled. Soon his chuckle grew until they were both rolling on the ground, tears running down their faces as they tried to control their giggles.

"What are they doing?" Miranda asked suddenly. She stood up and looked at the horses who had finally come to a stop beneath a tree near the top of a hill.

"Hey! They're making a baby!" Chris declared as he watched the black stallion rear above the sorrel mare.

"Oh, my gosh! Don't look, Chris. Stop that. Turn around."

"Why?"

"Well, that's private, that's why!"

Miranda's felt her face grow hot as she stood with her back to both Chris and the horses.

"Hey, he's ruining my saddle. How will I explain that to Dad?"

Miranda glanced back at the horses and saw

that Starlight's hoof was scraping down the side of the shiny black leather.

"Chris. Don't look," Miranda repeated. "Let's sit over there and eat our lunch. We have to figure out what to do next."

Chris agreed and the two sat with their backs against a rock that stood between them and the horses.

"We can't tell anyone about this, you know," Miranda said, suddenly aware that one secret was leading to the need for others. "I don't want people to know I brought Starlight out here. Not yet."

"They'll find out if Queen has a baby."

"Maybe not. They won't know it's from Starlight. Maybe they'll think she got in with Cadillac's Last Knight, or Dot's Dash, the quarter horse stallion."

"Mr. Taylor keeps both stallions in paddocks with ten foot high fences. There's no way she'd accidently get in with one of them."

"True," Miranda said, "Oh, well, she might not even be pregnant. We won't know for a long time."

"It's my saddle I'm worried about. Dad will have a fit when he sees it."

"We can put some black shoe polish on it so it won't show."

"Maybe. Let's go see if they're done fooling around and get back before someone comes."

The horses were standing a few feet apart, grazing, paying no attention to each other. However, as soon as Chris began leading Queen away, Starlight came to life. Miranda grabbed his halter rope and wrapped it around a tree branch.

"Go back without me. I'll wait until you're back to the stables before I bring Starlight."

Starlight whinnied and snorted as Queen trotted away from him, but he didn't try to break loose. Miranda continued to talk to him and tried to calm him down. When Chris disappeared behind the indoor arena, Miranda untied him and started back. He pranced and threw his head, but she managed to hold onto his halter rope and keep him from running away. She was almost to the indoor arena when she heard a car rumble across the cattle guard.

Ducking into the arena, Miranda hastily removed the saddle from the stallion and hid it behind the platform. Although she usually exercised him in the outdoor arena when the weather was nice, no one would think it strange that she chose to be indoors in the noonday heat. But then she looked at Starlight. He was completely wet with sweat and the imprint of the saddle was outlined in whitish foam. She remembered Adam's threat to turn Mr. Taylor against her and decided she couldn't risk upsetting either of them now. She looked around for something use to wipe the mark off Starlight's back. She couldn't find anything in the neat arena. One of the cardinal rules which Mr. Taylor strictly enforced was to keep everything in its place. Just outside the back door was a water hydrant with a short hose attached to it. She'd have to wash him.

She had helped give Queen a bath when they

spruced her up at the winter fair. She wished she had shampoo, a brush, and a sponge now as she had then, but she'd make do. She was wearing a T-shirt under her long-sleeved western plaid, which she wore unbuttoned. She took off both shirts, put the outer shirt back on, and buttoned it. The T-shirt would work as a wash cloth. She led Starlight out the back door and turned on the water. She showed it to him, speaking softly.

"I'm going to cool you off a bit, boy," she crooned. "It won't hurt. You'll love it."

She wet the shirt and wiped it over his chest. He stood still. She soaked it again and reached up to wipe it over his shoulder. The door at the other end of the arena opened and slammed shut. Miranda panicked. She had to erase the obvious signs of sweat and the mark of the saddle before anyone saw him. She sprayed the hose on his back, dousing him as fast as she could. Starlight snorted and reared, jerking the rope from Miranda's hand as he wheeled and tore across the pasture. He disappeared over a hill.

"What happened? Why did you let Starlight loose?" asked Chris, startling her.

"I was trying to wash him before someone saw him all sweated up," Miranda said, tears welling up in her eyes. "I heard someone drive in. Are Adam and Mr. Taylor back?"

"It was UPS," Chris told her.

"Is that all?" Miranda moaned. "I feel so stupid! Now, I've got to get him back before they do come!"

"I'll help. We've got an hour until Mom comes."

An hour and a half later, Miranda and Chris trudged back to the stables. Mrs. Bergman jumped out of her car and strode toward them as fast as she could in her high-heeled shoes.

"Where on earth have you been?" she shouted. "I was about to call out a search party. I looked in all the stables, the barn, the arena, and I even checked both Mr. Taylor's and Higgins' houses. There isn't a soul on this place. I thought you said you wouldn't be alone!"

"We didn't know everyone was going to leave," Miranda said meekly.

"Why didn't you come when I honked?" Mrs. Bergman asked, angrily. "Where were you?"

"We came as fast as we could. We were way back in the hill pasture..." Chris's voice trailed off, uncertainly.

"It's all my fault," Miranda said. "Starlight got away from me and Chris offered to help me try to catch him."

Mrs. Bergman was still lecturing them when Higgins and his nephew arrived. They agreed to help Miranda find the wayward stallion. Miranda phoned Grandma who said she could stay if she promised not to go anywhere or do anything without Higgins' permission. Mrs. Bergman and Chris hurried away.

The jeep bounced over the rough pasture, throwing Higgins half out of his seat when one front tire hit a rock his nephew hadn't seen. Miranda's head hit the roll-bar as she leaned forward from the back seat.

"Oops, sorry!" Higgins' nephew said. "I was looking up there on the hill by the trees. Isn't that a horse?"

"Sure is!" shouted Higgins. "It looks like he's found the fillies."

"What fillies?" Miranda asked in alarm.

"Mr. Taylor keeps the yearlings and two-year-old fillies in this pasture until we're ready to start their training. He keeps them away from the stallions until they're three years old.

"Oh, no! It might be too late. It looks like Starlight's rounding them up!" Miranda exclaimed.

"I think he's cutting one out from the rest of the herd. She must be in season," Higgins observed. "Come on, John. Let's see if we can chase him back to the barn with the jeep."

Chapter Six

It was a wild ride, as the topless four-wheel-drive vehicle clawed its way over roots, rocks, and sagebrush to the top of the hill. With the horn blaring, they headed straight for Starlight. Before they could get there, he dashed after the bay filly that fled behind the small band of horses running over the top of the hill and disappearing from sight.

"Oh, hurry," Miranda begged as she held on to the roll bar to keep from being thrown out.

The jeep slammed to a stop and backed up to avoid a tree, then eased forward over a large rock.

"I don't think we'll ever catch them. I can't drive faster than a crawl in this terrain," John said.

"There is a road, of sorts, over that way. It goes down to the pond, which is the only watering hole in this pasture," Higgins said, motioning to their left. "If you can find a way across that little ravine, you

can get on it and make better time."

"Hold on, then. I don't want to break your hip again," John said. "Here we go!"

"I'm so sorry I let him get away from me!" Miranda exclaimed, suddenly afraid that Higgins would be hurt again because of her mistake.

"I'll be all right," Higgins said. "Let's just get that horse of yours back where he belongs."

Miranda's heart skipped a beat at the sound of those words. Higgins must really think of Starlight as her horse! As they neared the pond, they saw a small group of fillies drinking from it. Several more stood off to one side looking toward a willow thicket, their ears pricked forward, necks arched. Miranda couldn't see Starlight. John eased the jeep forward as they all peered into the shadows of the trees. They heard a horse squeal and a bay filly dashed out to join the others. The jeep came to a stop, and Miranda jumped out. She jogged toward the thicket.

Starlight stood watching her, curious but not alarmed. She called his name softly as she walked toward him. He put his head down and sniffed the ground as if no longer interested. At last, he came to meet her.

"Well you naughty boy; are you ready to go home?" she asked as she grasped the frayed halter rope and let him eat sugar cubes from her hand.

He nudged her with his muzzle, looking for more. She laughed and dug another one from her pocket before leading him to the jeep. She noticed that Higgins was staring at Starlight. Miranda looked back and saw that a dirty saddle print showed plainly in his stiffly dried hair.

"If you sit in the back of the jeep and lead him, I think he'll follow. John will drive slow. If he jerks back let us know. Don't let him pull you out of the jeep. Let go first."

Miranda was relieved that Higgins said nothing about the saddle mark. Maybe he hadn't noticed it after all. Starlight followed willingly as Miranda fed him more treats, and they were back at the stables by six o'clock.

"Better give him a good brushing before Mr. Taylor gets home. The lad doesn't look at all presentable," Higgins said with a wink.

Mr. Taylor and Adam had not yet arrived when Miranda finished. Starlight's coat was shining and smooth by the time Grandma came to take Miranda home.

As Miranda did her chores the next morning, she heard a faint but distant whimper. She stopped halfway to the chicken house with a bucket of feed in one hand and a bucket of water in the other. She stood still, straining her ears. Hearing nothing, she walked on. Before she opened the chicken house door, she heard it again, louder this time. She put down her load and walked around the chicken house into the tall weeds that grew along the fence that divided their farm from the county road.

She looked hard, pulling back the weeds and brambles, stopping occasionally to listen. She heard a rustle in the dry leaves and saw a tiny black form. The woven wire fence stood in her way. She climbed over, but not without snagging her shirt. She yanked it loose, tearing a hole in the sleeve. Falling to her knees, she reached under the wild rose bush where she had seen the ball of black fur. After scratching her arm, hand, and face, she finally touched something soft and warm. Carefully she pulled the squirming, scratching fur ball from its hiding place. It was a puppy, no bigger than a football. As she held it to her chest, it licked her fingers. She carressed its head and its tight swollen belly as she scrambled onto the road and walked back to the house.

"Grandma, look what I found!" Miranda shouted as she hurried into the kitchen. "May I keep it? Please?"

"What is it? Let me see," Grandma said, gently taking it from her and turning it over to inspect it.

"He can't be more than five weeks old, and he's nearly starved! Someone must have dumped him," grandma exclaimed indignantly. "Get a bowl of milk and we'll see if we can teach him to drink."

Miranda dipped her fingers in the milk and let him lick it off while Grandma continued to hold him.

"Now do it again and lower your finger into the milk while he's licking it," Grandma instructed.

After a couple tries, the puppy got the idea and eagerly lapped the milk.

"He acts like he can't get it fast enough," Miranda laughed.

As they eased the puppy and the bowl to the floor, he never missed a lick, but went on lapping up milk like his life depended on it. It probably did.

"What's this?" asked Grandpa as he came in from the barn with a clean pail of fresh milk.

"I found him behind the chicken house by the road," Miranda said. "Isn't he darling?"

"Better not let him have too much at once," Grandpa warned, stooping to pick him up. "Well, well, little brother, where did you come from? Looks like Miranda found you just in time. Well, don't worry. We'll see that you don't go hungry again."

"Little Brother!" Miranda exclaimed, laughing

as she reached for him. "What a cute name for him, Grandpa. Thanks for letting me keep him."

"Letting YOU keep him?" Grandpa teased. "He'll be our dog. This farm has been needing a dog ever since old Shag died two years ago."

"Breakfast is ready, and then I'd like you to start the laundry, Miranda," Grandma said. "I want to set some bread to rise before I drive you and Chris to Shady Hills. You do have your chores done, don't you?"

"Oh, I forgot my chickens and rabbits!" Miranda shouted as she dashed out the door.

She apologized to her pets, but finished quickly and hurried back to help Grandma.

She was putting the load of white clothes in the washer when the phone rang.

"Miranda, it's for you."

"Hello?"

"When are you coming over? Aren't you coming today?"

Miranda jumped when she heard Mr. Taylor's gruff voice. He had never called her at home, or even gone out of his way to speak to her before. She could hardly breathe. *Someone told him about yesterday,* she thought in dismay. She gulped, gripped the phone and looked at Grandma.

"Yes, I, uh... I have to help Grandma for a little while. Then she'll bring me."

"Can you bring a cake?"

"A cake?" Miranda asked.

"That's what I said." Mr. Taylor sounded angry. "I danged near forgot Elliot's birthday. I think it hurt his feelings."

"Oh, I see," Miranda said, realizing that Mr. Taylor wasn't angry. He was embarrassed.

"I don't want him to think I don't care. It just slipped my mind this morning. If you bring a cake, we'll have a little party at lunch time."

"I'll make a cake, and maybe we can pick up some party things. I'll bring the present I got for him."

With Grandma's help, the cake was baked and decorated by the time the second load of laundry was hung outside on the clothes line. It was after ten when they stopped at Bergman's general store, and Chris was waiting impatiently. When he heard about the birthday party, he went back for a gift. After delivering the cake, Grandma offered to make a big pizza for the party and to bring Mark, Elliot's best friend.

"I'll be back before you know it," Grandma said, when Mr. Taylor protested that it was too much to ask.

Miranda hugged her and whispered, "Thanks." At least one grownup had some idea of what a little boy might like on his birthday.

True to her promise, Grandma was soon back with pizza, pop, and not only Mark, but Laurie, too. When the pizza was gone, Miranda lit the seven candles on the birthday cake.

"Make a wish before you blow them out," Mark prompted.

Elliot closed his eyes for a long moment before blowing out all of them.

"What did you wish for?" Mark asked.

"I can't tell or it won't come true," Elliot said.

There were five packages on the cupboard, and Chris handed one to Elliot.

"I didn't have time to do much shopping, but Dad let me pick something out from his store. I think you'll like it."

"Oh, this is so cool!" Elliot exclaimed. "Look, Grandfather, a pocket knife with all kinds of blades and things. Look, there is even a little pair of scissors and a screwdriver! Thank you, Chris."

"I didn't have time to buy you anything, but I thought you wouldn't mind if I gave you something of mine," said Mark as he brought a small brown paper bag to Elliot.

"Of course I don't. That just makes it more special," Elliot assured him as he looked inside the sack. "Oh, wow! Thank you, Mark. Your buffalo nickels! Are you sure you want..."

"I want you to have them, if you want them," said Mark. "You're my best friend."

"I'll keep them in my treasure box forever, and that way I'll always remember what a good friend you are," Elliot said earnestly.

Laurie had chosen and wrapped one of the model horses from her collection. Elliot opened it next and thanked Laurie with a smile

"It looks a lot like Sunny," he said.

"Here. This one's from me," said Miranda.

When Elliot pulled out a pair of cowboy boots, he shouted and gave Miranda a hug.

"May I try them on right now?" he asked.

"Sure. If they don't fit, I can take them back."

"They fit perfectly," he said as he strutted around the kitchen.

Miranda was glad she saved the money she got for her own birthday. She had seen the boots when shopping with Grandma one day.

"Well, aren't you going to open the one from me?" asked Mr. Taylor.

Elliot slowly opened the last and biggest package. His face was solemn as he pulled out a model race car.

"How cool!" exclaimed Mark, peering into the box and pulling out a radio control. "Let's try it out."

"Okay," Elliot agreed halfheartedly. "Thank you, Grandfather."

Miranda looked quickly at Mr. Taylor. He looked sad. She guessed that even he could see that Elliot had been disappointed in his gift.

"Oh, there are no batteries," said Mark. "Do you have any, Mr. Taylor."

"I don't know. What size does it take?" he asked gruffly, seizing the remote control from Mark.

"It takes a nine volt and four D batteries," Chris told them.

"Well, I don't have any nine volt batteries," said Mr. Taylor. "Why don't they make them so they take just one size?"

"It's okay, Grandfather," Elliot said. "We can get some later."

Chapter Seven

This wasn't turning out to be the happy birthday Miranda had hoped for Elliot. Mr. Taylor was sullen. Elliot seemed near tears, and no one else seemed to know what to do with themselves. Desperate to break the awkward silence, Miranda started clearing the table, and Laurie helped her.

Mark looked at Elliot questioningly. "Do you want to go outside and play?"

"I guess so," Elliot said.

"Wait! There's one more thing, Elliot," Mr. Taylor said. "I'll be back in a minute."

He disappeared into his den.

"I'll help you, Miranda," Elliot offered.

"Okay, if you want to. It's your birthday, though."

Elliot glanced at Chris and Mark who were looking at the new Swiss army knife and exclaiming over all the features.

"I don't think Grandfather remembered that it was my birthday this morning," Elliot confided. "He yelled at me for being so glum, and I started crying. I couldn't help it. I miss Mum so bad. We used to do such special things on our birthdays; something different every year."

"Mr. Taylor doesn't know how to be a good mother, that's for sure," Miranda whispered, "but I think he's trying."

"I know he is. I'm afraid I didn't look very happy about the car. It's a nice present, I just..."

"I know,"Miranda whispered. "It wasn't what you hoped for."

"I tried to give him some hints, and I thought he might..." Elliot began.

He fell silent when he heard Mr. Taylor 's footsteps.

"Here's the rest of your birthday present, Elliot. I don't know if you'll like it, but, well here."

He held out a plain white envelope. Elliot took it uncertainly and turned it over. There was nothing written on it. He opened it slowly, looking as if he feared it held a bomb.

"Oh, Wow! Oh, Grandfather, Oh, wow-o-wow-o-wow!" Elliot exclaimed, falling to his knees on the floor.

Tears streamed down his face and he began laughing hysterically. "Oh, Grandfather, you gave me my wish! Thank you, thank you. How did you know what I wanted?"

"Are you all right, m'boy? Why are you crying? Or are you laughing? Just tell me, do you like it or not?"

"It's the best present in the world. It's what I wished for with all my heart," said Elliot as he ran to his Grandfather and hugged him.

Miranda scooped the folded document from the floor. "Sundance Queen," she read on the registration paper. "Elliot Montgomery" was penned in Mr. Taylor's bold handwriting in the transfer of ownership form on the back. Sunny, as they called her, was Elliot's favorite horse.

The day was nearly over before Miranda had a chance to go see Starlight. When she went to his stall, she met Adam coming out with a halter in his hand.

"What were you doing with my horse?" she asked accusingly.

"Your horse?"

"With Starlight. You know who I mean. What were you doing?"

"Don't get all worked up, Half-pint. You know it's my job to train Mr. Taylor's horses. Sir Jet Propelled Cadillac," he emphasized the name with a sarcastic tone, "is one of Mr. Taylor's horses and the most urgent to train. He's three years old, Miranda. Taylor told me to start working him a little everyday."

Miranda frowned at the sound of Starlight's

full registered name.

"Starlight," she said, emphasizing the name, "get's exercised every day. I've been doing just what Mr. Taylor told me to do."

And more, she thought. Although she knew that Starlight was not officially her horse, she hated for anyone else to work with him.

"I told you before, Miranda, he's ready for a professional trainer now. I don't want you to do any more than lead him around. Do you understand? If it were my horse, I wouldn't let any kids mess with him at all."

Miranda's temper had reached the boiling point as Adam disappeared into the tack shed to put the halter away. She wished Adam had never come to Shady Hills and into her life. He treated her like a baby. If he wasn't actually finding some fault, he was making a belittling remark or bossing her around.

I'll show him, she thought. *Starlight may not be mine on paper, but his heart belongs to me.*

She found Starlight in the lower end of his paddock looking out into the pasture, and for a moment she wanted to just open the gate and let him run wild and free. But remembering the trouble that had come the last time she accidentally left his gate ajar, she realized that freedom had a price. She wouldn't risk his safety again.

When she called to him, Starlight looked her way and took a few steps in her direction. He stopped to nibble a little grass and then looked toward

Miranda again.

"Are you playing hard-to-get?" laughed Miranda. "Come here, boy, give me a break!"

Miranda held a carrot out to him and he tossed his head playfully and trotted to her. Taking it from her hand, he shook it comically before biting into it. Miranda ran to the other end of the paddock and whistled. He came trotting as she had been teaching him to do. This time, instead of rewarding him with more treats, she just stroked his neck. He soon tired of that and spun around, bucking and twisting as he ran toward the stable. When Miranda didn't follow, he stopped and whinnied. Miranda laughed.

He followed her into the stall and she closed the door to his paddock. Looking out the front door, Miranda saw that Adam was in the round pen working with a sorrel gelding who was half-brother to Queen. She had heard Mr. Taylor tell him he wanted this one ready for the upcoming race in Great Falls. It looked to her like Adam had a lot of work to do, if that was going to happen. She was about to close the door when Chris stepped out of Queen's stall and called to her.

"Want to come watch me ride?"

"No."

"Ah, come on. It's much more fun when someone's with me."

"We don't dare put Starlight and Queen together for awhile, and I want to work with Starlight. Go ahead and ride. Maybe we can play in the old barn later."

She would rather ride down by the river, or up to the cave, but riding double wasn't her favorite thing to do. She wished Mr. Taylor would offer to let her ride one of his other horses, but he didn't and she wouldn't ask. She didn't have the money he charged to rent one.

The hay loft of the old barn was one of their favorite places. There were still a few remaining piles of loose hay here and there, and a stack of bales. In the days before balers, the ranchers lifted the hay from wagons with a big hook on ropes and pulleys to store in the loft of the barn. The rope was still there and made a wonderful trapeze as they swung from one side of the barn to the other. Trying to outdo each other, she and Chris would perform stunts like hanging upside down, spinning around, and doing flips into the piles of loose hay.

But for now, Miranda just wanted to have some time alone with Starlight. She got a soft brush from the tack shed when she went after his halter. Starlight stood contentedly, pressing against her hand as she brushed him from head to tail and down each leg. She led him out into the paddock next to the white board fence. Standing between him and the fence, she stepped up the rails backward, scratching his back as she climbed. When she was high enough, she lowered herself slowly onto his back.

Her heart pounded as she felt his muscles tighten. His head lifted and one ear flicked back. She patted his neck and spoke softly until he relaxed. Squeezing her legs slightly, and shifting her weight forward, she sent a subtle signal to Starlight. He stepped forward, slowly at first and then faster. Miranda didn't pull back on the halter rope, but sat back comfortably, careful not to clamp down with her legs. Starlight slowed, and as Miranda leaned back and gently pulled on the halter rope, Starlight stopped.

Miranda wanted to shout and cheer, but she only smiled and patted his withers.

"Good boy," she said. "You are the smartest horse in the world."

He was responding to her cues! They understood each other as well as if they spoke the same language. Maybe they did; the language of love. How different this was from the first time she'd gotten on him. Less than a year ago, she'd tried to mount him out in the field near the school. He'd jumped away and dumped her on the ground. So much had happened since then that it seemed like years ago. When she had gotten on him again a few weeks later, she'd been thrown again, but Starlight had suffered most. She had feared that his terrible experience in the bog; tangled, trapped, and torn by barbed-wire, would make him wild for the rest of his life — if he survived the physical cuts and infection. But he did survive, and he was gentle and devoted to her because of their closeness through his long months of healing.

Miranda pulled the rope to her left, bringing Starlight's head around as she slightly shifted her weight forward and pressed her right leg against his side. He responded immediately, turning and trotting up the paddock to the stable.

"Miranda?" She heard Elliot call from the other side of the stable row.

Sitting back and tightening Starlight's halter rope, she managed to slow him to a walk as she swung her right leg over his back and dropped to the ground. She fell to her hands and knees, but jumped up and walked beside Starlight's head. She hoped that she appeared only to be leading him as Elliot came through the stable into the paddock. The fewer people who knew her secret, the better.

"Your grandmother's here. She wants you to go now." Elliot said, eyeing her suspiciously.

Grandpa met them as they stopped the car in front of the garage.

"Get in the truck with me, Mandy. The cows got through the fence into Caruthers' pasture. I need your help in getting them back."

They drove down the county road three miles to Caruthers' farmstead. Old Mr. Caruthers met them and offered to open and close the first gate across a narrow lane that led to his river pasture. When Grandpa stopped at the next gate, made of barbed wire, Miranda jumped out to open it so Grandpa could ease the truck through. She struggled to close it, but it was too tight. Grandpa closed it for her. The cows were scattered among the willows, grazing on the lush grass.

"I'll drive over there where they broke through the fence. I'll have to cut the two wires that are left so they'll go through," said Grandpa. "Then you can take them back to the barn while I fix the fence."

The big holstein cows looked at Miranda warily and ran through the brush in all directions as she approached.

"You stupid cows are acting like you never saw me before. Now get back where you belong!" Miranda shouted. "If I just had Starlight here, you wouldn't be able to hide from me. This place needs a good horse!"

Grandpa soon joined her, and together they crowded the cows through the opening in the fence. Miranda had to keep them going toward the barn. As they got closer, it was easier to keep them together and moving, for they were used to being herded in for milking every afternoon.

Miranda woke suddenly to a sharp bark, right in her ear, followed by whines and scratching at the door. Miranda had dozed off to sleep with Little Brother curled up on the bed beside her. Now he was frantically trying to get out of her room, running from window to door. Miranda jumped up and opened the door for him, dashing behind him to let him out the back door of the house. She flipped on the yard light, hurried outside, and saw the black puppy streaking toward the chicken house.

"Oh no," Miranda gasped. "I forgot to shut up the chickens."

Chapter Eight

Grandpa caught up with Miranda just as they rounded the granary. He had a shot gun in his hand. It was hard to see, as the granary blocked the glow of the yard light. The heard of chickens squawking, wings flapping, and Little Brother's frantic barking.

A beam of light shone on the side of the chicken house where an eighteen inch high door opened into the wire mesh enclosure. Grandma stood beside Miranda with a flashlight. Something gray and furry streaked across the yard and struggled for just a moment through a hole under the fence. As Grandpa raised his gun to his shoulder, the coyote disappeared into the darkness.

Little Brother came bounding out of the chicken house, a frightened rooster flapping and squawking before him. Ignoring the chicken, Little Brother took off after the coyote.

"Well, let's see how much damage it did," said Grandma.

But Miranda was already running.

"Here Barkley," Miranda called. "Chick, chick, chick. Here, boy, don't be afraid."

The rooster ran to the side of the fence, but stopped, lowered his back, and made a frightened, low pitched garble as Miranda put her hand on his back. She picked him up and cradled him in her arms. Grandma was already in the doorway, shining her flashlight beam inside. Red and white feathers were scattered across the floor and the hens milled around, for a moment before hopping back onto the roost.

"One, two, three four, five. Oh there's another one, under the rabbit hutch." Miranda said, as she gently placed Barkley on the roost and knelt beside the speckled hen.

"Is she all right?" asked Grandpa. "That's all of them, isn't it?"

"She's lost some feathers. Her tail is almost bare," Miranda said. "But she isn't bleeding anywhere. I think she's just scared. Poor Minnie."

Miranda lifted the hen and hugged her close. She could feel the chicken's rapid pulse beneath her hand.

"Well, looks like we're pretty lucky," Grandpa said. "They're all here and in one piece, if we don't count the feathers."

"Thanks to Little Brother," added Grandma.

"I could have lost them all, just because I forgot about them tonight," Miranda said. "I'm sorry. It won't happen again."

"Where is Little Brother?" asked Grandma.

They searched and called, but finally gave up and went to bed. But Miranda couldn't sleep for worrying about the brave puppy who had been with them for such a short time. She kept getting up and going to the door to call his name. *The coyote is much bigger than he is,* she thought. *What if he turns on Little brother? My puppy won't stand a chance.* Unable to stand it any longer, Miranda dressed, grabbed a flashlight, and went out to find him.

She walked past the granary, the chicken house, and finally the milk barn, calling as she went. She heard one short bark, and then whining. Following the sound she soon found him. He'd wandered into the calf pen, got caught behind the wooden feeder, and couldn't find his way back to the house. It was hard to tell who was the happiest, Miranda or Little Brother, when she scooped him up and carried him back to the house.

Early Friday morning, Miranda finished wiping the last dish and put it away as Grandma opened the door for Mrs. Langley and Laurie.

"I know I'm a little early, but I had to get up early to see Preston off. He left for a sales trip to the coast. Laurie talked me into riding with her today since I was already up and about."

How fun, Miranda thought. *If I only had a horse;*

if Starlight was mine, I could go with them.

"Miranda has all her chores done," said Grandma. "I'll help her fix her lunch so you can be on your way."

"Oh, no hurry. I doubt Chris will be ready yet," said Mrs. Langley.

"I'll call and tell him we're coming," said Miranda.

"I'll help you fix your lunch," offered Laurie.

"May I get you some coffee?" asked Grandma, reaching for the pot on the stove.

The grownups sat and drank coffee as the girls fixed lunch and tidied up the kitchen.

"I should probably call and make sure Mr. Taylor has a horse I can rent for the day," Mrs. Langley said before they left. "May I use your phone?"

Grandma handed her the cordless.

"Yes," Mrs. Langley said into the phone. "I'd love to ride Cinder again. And Miranda needs a horse. Could I rent the one Preston rode?... Why thank you, Mr. Taylor... Sure. We'd love to have Elliot come along."

"You rented a horse for me?" Miranda asked in surprise. "Thank you. I'll pay you back."

"No need. That sweet man refused to let us pay for either of them today," Mrs. Langley said. "All he asks is that we let Elliot come along and that I keep a close watch over him."

The ride along the river through the willows

and cottonwoods was just what Miranda had been longing for. They crossed a shallow stream that ran into the river.

"This is where I went over Starlight's head the day he got hurt," Miranda told Laurie.

"My goodness," her friend answered. "It's a wonder you didn't get killed; it's so rocky!"

"Yeah, I was lucky, I guess, but poor Starlight wasn't. Right behind those willows is where he got wallowed down in the bog and tangled up in wire."

She shuddered at the memory of the young black stallion's terrified screams and wild eyes as he struggled in the thick black mud.

After a slow, but pleasant ride along the river, they ate their lunches in a meadow of wild flowers.

"I think Sunny is the prettiest horse in the world. Don't you Chris?" Elliot asked.

"She's no prettier than Queen!" Chris declared. "They sure do look a lot alike, though, don't they."

"Lady is the nicest." Laurie said. "I told you I'd name my first horse Moon Beam to go with Starlight, Miranda. But since Lady already has a name, it'll have to be her foal, if she ever has one. Mr. Taylor doesn't think she can. That's why he sold her."

Miranda listened to her friends go on and on about their horses. She started to say that she thought Starlight was the prettiest and best of all, but tears filled her eyes and a lump blocked her throat as she realized she might never be able to call him her own. She rose and walked to where Fortune, the gray gelding was munching grass. Hiding her face from her friends, she took off his halter and put the bridle on.

"What's your hurry, Miranda. Some of us aren't through eating yet," Chris said. "Hey, neither are you. You left half a sandwich, some cookies, and half of your apple."

"You can have my sandwich and cookies. Fortune gets the rest of my apple," Miranda said in as normal a voice as she could muster.

She snatched up the apple without looking at Chris.

"What's wrong, Miranda?" Laurie asked. "You aren't going yet, are you?"

"I'm just going to explore a little while the rest of you finish eating."

Miranda felt she must get away to let the tears fall unseen. She didn't feel like talking to anyone.

"Wait, I'll come with you," said Laurie.

"That's okay. I'll be back," Miranda said quickly, climbing into the saddle and turning away.

"Don't go far," called Mrs. Langley. "We'll be through in a few minutes."

As soon as she was out of sight of the others. Miranda let the tears fall unheeded. *Am I jealous of my friends?* she asked herself as she wound her way through trees and bushes. *No,* she thought. *I don't want them to have any less than what they have. I just want Starlight, and it doesn't look like I'll ever get to buy him.* Her dreams of owning him, starting a horse ranch with Laurie, and raising race horses seemed so unlikely just now that she couldn't help feeling sad. Maybe Laurie would have the ranch without her.

"Mr. Taylor would have had Starlight killed if it hadn't been for me, so why won't he let me have him now?" She muttered as tears stung her eyes.

Overcome with anger at this injustice, she brought her tight fist down on Fortune's withers.

Fortune jumped sideways before breaking into a run. Caught by surprise, Miranda grabbed the saddle horn and then buried her face in Fortune's mane as he threw his head up. She almost lost her balance again when he lunged forward, but pulled herself upright and held on. She had dropped one rein, but pulled back on the other one. Fortune turned and stepped on the rein that was dragging on the ground, snapping it in two with a sudden jerk of his head.

Fortune stopped so suddenly that Miranda was thrown onto his neck, somersaulted over his head, and landed on her back at his feet. Her helmet was askew, covering one eye. She straightened it as she stood and picked up the remaining rein. Fortune trembled, but didn't move. He was wet with sweat.

"I'm so sorry, Fortune," Miranda said, aghast at the realization that she had struck a horse! "I never meant to hit you."

She was as shaky as the horse. She led him back the way they came, looking for the broken rein as she walked. She found it and tried to tie it back on but in a little while it came undone.

"I guess I'll just have to keep leading you," she told Fortune.

Shaken from the fall and horrified at what her quick temper had led her to do, she was not anxious to get back on. She walked on, head down, blinded by tears as she tried to sort out her feelings.

"I don't deserve a horse if I can't control my temper any better than that," she murmured, scolding herself.

Wiping her eyes, she looked around. She had never been in this part of the pasture before. She didn't know which way they had entered the small clearing where she had fallen. Her head throbbed and her back hurt.

"We must have come through that opening," Miranda told Fortune.

Talking to the horse helped her feel less lonely and afraid. Fortune followed obediently and unconcerned, but the opening only led to a thick wall of brush.

She turned right and wound around trees and bushes until she came to a wide slough that she had never seen before.

"Laurie!" Miranda shouted, "Chris! Elliot!"

There was no answer; no sound at all.

Chapter Nine

Miranda turned around and hurried in the direction she'd come. She trudged through thick grass and around trees and bushes. When she couldn't find the clearing where she had fallen, she admitted she was lost.

"You don't seem at all worried, or in any hurry to go home," she told Fortune who was complacently chomping a mouthful of grass.

A rumble in the distance caused Miranda to look up. Dark clouds covered half the sky.

"We'd better find shelter or we're going to get wet. I don't know the way back, so I'm going to leave it up to you."

Miranda had read stories about horses taking their hopelessly lost masters safely home on dark, stormy nights. Maybe Fortune could do it for her in the day time. She got back into the saddle and with the one rein slack, she urged him forward.

"Come on, Fortune. Take us home."

Given his head, Fortune turned and strode off with a purpose in the direction opposite from the way they had been going. In a few minutes they came to the meadow where they had eaten lunch. No one was there.

"Laurie! Chris!" Miranda yelled again. This time she heard an answering call from up ahead.

"I'm back here," she shouted.

Soon Queen came into view from behind a large cottonwood tree and the others followed.

"Where were you?" Chris demanded.

"We looked and looked for you until we decided you must have circled around and gone back," Mrs. Langley said, sounding upset. "Didn't you hear us calling?"

"No. I'm sorry," Miranda apologized. "I went farther than I meant to."

A big drop of rain landed on Miranda's nose and then many more followed, pelting her back and shoulders and drumming on her helmet.

"Let's get under that big tree," said Mrs. Langley. "I don't think this will last long."

As they watched from the shelter of the cottonwood, the rain increased to a steady downpour.

"Miranda, I'm sorry I kept talking about my horse and about getting a colt." Laurie whispered, grasping Miranda's hand. "I didn't mean to be bragging. I should have thought about how it would make you feel."

"That's okay, Laurie. I wasn't mad at you. I just felt sad and wanted to be alone," Miranda whispered back. "I'm just afraid I'll never get Starlight for my own, and I love him so much."

"Miranda! What on earth did you do to your helmet? It has a crack in it," Grandma exclaimed as Miranda headed to the bathroom to brush her teeth before going to bed.

She stepped to the kitchen to see what Grandma was talking about. Grandma held up Miranda's riding helmet and pointed to a large crack in the back of it. Miranda knew it hadn't been there when she put the helmet on that morning.

"I didn't know it was there," Miranda said.

"Did you bump your head today? Did you fall off your horse?" Grandma sounded worried.

"Well," Miranda hesitated.

She hadn't planned to tell anyone. Falling off a horse was embarrassing for Miranda who prided herself in being an expert rider. Besides, she never knew what restrictions the grownups would put on her if she made a mistake and they found out about it.

"Miranda?"

"Well," she paused, drawing a deep breath. She couldn't lie to her grandparents anymore. "I did take a little tumble. I didn't realize it broke my helmet."

She wondered if she'd landed on a rock or hit Fortune's hoof as she fell. No wonder her head ached.

"What little tumble?" Grandma wouldn't let the subject die until she heard every detail, so Miranda told the whole story.

"You know you shouldn't have left the others. Not only was it dangerous; it was rude," Grandma scolded. "Just think what would have happened if you hadn't been wearing your helmet. You must not get on a horse again until I get you another one. Promise you won't or I'll keep you at home where I can watch you."

Relieved that she wasn't told she couldn't ride ever again, Miranda promised. She hoped Grandma would get her another one soon.

When Miranda arrived at Shady Hills, Adam had Starlight on a longe line on the lawn in front of the riding arena. Adam was flicking Starlight with a whip, to get the horse to circle around him. Starlight shook his head against the tug of the line and kicked backward each time the whip hit his hind quarters.

"Hey! You don't have to whip him, Adam. You're just making him mad," Miranda shouted as she jumped out of Grandma's Subaru.

"I'm not whipping him. I'm barely touching him with it. Now go mind your own business!" Adam yelled back.

"Starlight is my business," Miranda declared hotly.

Starlight skidded to a stop, tossed his head, jerked the longe line from Adam's hand, and trotted toward Miranda.

"Now look what you've done. I'm supposed to be training this horse and you're interfering."

Adam, who was red in the face, had never yelled at her so loudly. Starlight nudged her shirt pocket and she fed him a piece of carrot. Adam grabbed Starlight's halter and pulled him away.

"Now, get out of his sight and quit feeding him. After I talk to Cash Taylor, you won't be allowed to come near this horse until I'm done with his training," Adam said.

"You'll never be done with his training if you keep treating him like that!" Miranda yelled.

"Miranda," Grandma said, putting her hand on Miranda's arm. "Adam has been ordered to train Mr. Taylor's horse. You have to let him do it by his own methods."

Tears stung Miranda's eyes. She jerked free of Grandma's grasp and ran to the old barn. She climbed the ladder to the loft and flung herself into a pile of hay and sobbed. She didn't know how long she cried, but at last the tears were spent and she lay quietly, staring at the rafters. An occasional hiccup shook her body.

"Miranda?"

It was Chris. Miranda didn't feel like talking to anyone so she didn't answer.

"Miranda, I'm sorry. Adam can't begin to handle Starlight like you do."

Miranda opened her eyes to see Chris staring

at her.

"It's just not fair!" Miranda exclaimed, sitting up; tears falling again. "Starlight is mine and nobody knows it but Starlight and me."

"I hope you're not mad at me for coming up," Chris said. "Your grandma told us to leave you alone until you calmed down. She went riding with Laurie and Elliot, but I told them I didn't want to go."

"I don't mind. I'm glad you came." And suddenly she was.

"I was listening to Mr. Taylor tell Adam he wants him to go with him to a horse sale tomorrow. Elliot is going to Mark's house for the day."

"That's good. But your mother will be here."

"Not if we promise not to ride. She'll be glad to drop us off and get back to her own stuff."

"I can keep that promise. I can't ride until I get a helmet anyway, but Laurie will want to."

"She told me she's not coming tomorrow. She's going to Bozeman with her mother," Chris said.

"All right!" Miranda exclaimed, "I'll work with Starlight. I'll teach him how to longe and I can start driving him from the ground to teach him how to rein. That's how my grandpa taught the team we used to have when I was little. Hey! Maybe I can get Laurie's mom to pick up a helmet for me"

Mrs. Bergman seemed glad to leave Chris and Miranda at Shady Hills the next day. She checked with Higgins to be sure he was going to be home, made both of them promise not to ride, and hurried away.

Starlight nosed Miranda's shirt pocket for a treat. She laughed and pulled a bag of apple slices from her pocket and fed them to him. She put a halter on him and took him to the open lot near the arena where Adam had longed him the day before.

She led him in a circle, around and around, until he was going faster than she was and she trotted beside him. She let out more and more of the long lead rope and ran inside the circle as he trotted around her. She laughed and cheered him on, finally standing in the center of the circle, holding the very end of the halter rope. Starlight continued to trot in an eight foot circle around her.

"Good boy!" she exclaimed as she finally pulled him in to her. She gave him a sugar cube from her shirt pocket and asked Chris to bring the longe line. She snapped it on his halter in place of the lead rope and began moving him around the circle as she had before, gradually letting out more and more line until Starlight was trotting in a wide arc around her.

"Go, Starlight, go!" she shouted.

He responded to her excitement and was soon cantering around her.

"Whoa," she called, reeling in the longe line.

Starlight turned and trotted to her, ready for the sugar cube she held out for him.

"Now I'll try it the other direction," she said.

Starlight didn't fall into it as quickly this time, but fought bending to his right; first pulling against the line, then letting it drag the ground. Patiently, Miranda put the halter rope back on and led him in a circle with her hand near his nose on the halter rope. Very gradually she quickened her pace, and let more rope out as she fell back beside him. After a couple of tries, he was circling her as she pivoted at the end of his halter rope. Rewarding him again, she exchanged the halter rope for the longe line and started over. No longer fighting the curve to the right, he lengthened his stride and was soon trotting around her as she stood in the middle of a circle as big as the long longe line would allow.

"Go, Starlight. Let it all out!" Miranda yelled.

Starlight broke into an easy lope and continued to circle the girl who held his heart strings.

"Well, I'll be switched!"

Higgins voice broke into Miranda's concentration. She turned abruptly to stare at the old man leaning on his walker. Starlight slowed as the longe line slackened and dragged the ground. Taking that as a signal, he walked to Miranda and searched her pocket for a treat. She gave him one and patted his nose as she looked at Higgins.

"Adam said he couldn't get Sir Jet to do anything but fight the longe line and kick at the whip. He said he never felt so much like beating a horse in his life," Higgins said. "I told him that never did a horse any good at all. Maybe you could give Adam some pointers. You know how to work with a horse instead of against it."

"Thanks, Higgins, but Adam wouldn't listen to me if his life depended on it," Miranda said. "Please don't tell him what I did today. He'd just tell Mr. Taylor to make me stay away from Starlight."

Miranda stood stroking the stallion's neck until she saw his ears prick up. She heard a car coming down the gravel road.

Chapter Ten

Higgins looked up at the road and said to Miranda, "I see a cloud of dust just over the hill. Adam must be driving. Are you sure you don't want to show them what your Starlight will do for you?"

"Oh, no. Please don't tell. Here, Chris, would you please put the longe line back while I put Starlight in his paddock?"

After Mr. Taylor parked his Cadillac in the garage, he and Adam walked over to Higgins.

"You're looking pretty spry. Out for your daily stroll?" asked Mr. Taylor.

"Yeah. It gets kind of dull sitting in the house playing solitaire and watching the tube. Besides, I like looking over the place once in awhile. You never know what kind of excitement an old guy like me might run into."

"I don't know what there is to excite anybody

around here," said Adam, looking around.

"How does the place look to you?" asked Mr. Taylor, "Is Adam doing his job?"

"Well, there's an awful lot for one man to do," Higgins said. "I'd like to see him spend a little more time on Roman Candle if you want to have him ready to race in Great Falls."

"He's ready!" Adam said. "What about Sir Jet? How am I supposed to have him ready to race this fall if I don't spend most of my time with him?"

"Well, I wouldn't worry about Sir Jet until after Great Falls," Higgins said. "If you don't keep at it every day, Roman Candle won't stay ready."

"You heard the old man," Mr. Taylor said. "Spend your time on Roman Candle for now."

Miranda stayed in Starlight's stall until Adam and Mr. Taylor walked by on their way to the house. When they were past, she came out with a fork full of shavings and dumped them into a wheel barrow.

"What are you doing here?" Adam asked, turning to glare at her.

"Cleaning Starlight's stall, why?"

"That horse has the cleanest stall, freshest water and shiniest coat of any horse on the place," Higgins commented, walking toward her.

"She's a mighty good worker for such a little thing," Mr. Taylor agreed, turning and walking back toward her. "She's done wonders with that horse."

"More than you can imagine," Higgins said with a wink at Miranda.

"She's spoiled him," Adam argued. "I think he'd be easier to work with if he wasn't coddled so much!"

"Oh, I don't know that I've ever seen a horse spoiled by kind attention," said Higgins, "and I've seen a lot of horses in my day. It's mistreatment that hurts them."

"Miranda, come here," Mr. Taylor ordered as she went back into the stall for another fork full of shavings. "I've been meaning to pay you for baby sitting. You should have reminded me."

Miranda stared at the fifty dollar bill Mr. Taylor held out to her.

"You don't owe me that much. I only stayed with Elliot twice."

"I owe you more than that for cleaning stalls and taking care of Sir Jet, not to mention all the work you did to help Higgins when he was suffering from a bad back last winter."

"Thank you very much," she said, taking the money. "I'd be glad to clean stalls for you every day. But you can't pay me for taking care of Starlight. He's my responsibility."

"Nonsense!" Mr. Taylor said. "There aren't many stalls to clean now that most of the horses are out on summer pasture, but I'll pay you to help Elliot take care of Sunny. I hope you won't spend your money foolishly."

"Oh, I won't," Miranda said. "I'll put it all in the bank. I'm saving to buy a horse."

"Oh, I see. Let me know when you're ready and I'll help you pick out a good one."

"I have one picked out," Miranda said.

"Oh, do you? What horse is that?"

"Starlight."

"Oh, I'm afraid you won't save that much money in a very long time. If he wins his first race, I'm taking him to Denver to run, then on to California. Once he has a few wins to his name, he'll be ready to take Knight's place as our top thoroughbred stud."

"But Mr. Taylor," Miranda said, clutching his hand, "He has scars. You said he'd never be any good for racing or breeding. But he's great for me. He'll do anything for me."

"Well a man can be wrong. Doctor Talbot has me believing this horse might live up to his full potential in spite of the scars," Mr. Taylor said.

"You wouldn't even have him if I hadn't talked you into saving him. You were going to have him put down!" Miranda was near tears, but determined to plead her case.

"Yes, I know, and I'm very glad you talked me into it, but I bred him to take Knight's place. Knight will be too old in another year or two. Now I'm convinced I was right about Sir Jet. I think he's the perfect replacement for the old boy."

"But, why Starlight? There are tons of other colts on this ranch," Miranda protested.

"Shady Hills has a reputation for having a jet black stud that breeds true. People who want a black horse will pay a mighty good price to have their mares bred to such a horse. Why, people come from all over the country," Mr. Taylor boasted. "You'd better be looking for another horse to buy."

Cadillac's Last Knight was a blue-black stallion. His son, Starlight had the same irridescent sheen, just like a raven's feather.

Early the next morning, Miranda was surprised by a knock on the door. When she saw it was her friend Laurie, she invited her into the kitchen.

"Here's your new helmet, Miranda. I tried it on and I, well I hope you like it," Laurie's voice trailed off as she stared at Miranda. "Is there something wrong with it?"

Miranda stared soberly at the black riding helmet. She took a deep breath and let it out slowly before she answered.

"It's nice, Laurie. Thank you." Setting it on the table, Miranda continued. "Did you have enough money?"

"Oh, yes. There was a little left over. Here."

Miranda took the money that Laurie held out to her and laid it beside the helmet. When Miranda still didn't respond, Laurie asked, "You don't like it?"

"I do. I like it better than my old one," Miranda said. "It's just... I'm not going to Shady Hills today. I was going to call so your mother wouldn't have to drive over here."

"But Miranda," Laurie asked in surprise, "why

not?"

"I have too much to do. I haven't cleaned the chicken house or rabbit cages for weeks. They're an awful mess."

"I'll help you this afternoon when we get back. I don't want to go without you. Please?" Laurie begged.

"I don't want to go," Miranda replied her voice sharper than she meant it to be.

"Miranda, are you still mad at me for the other day?" Tears welled up in Laurie's brown eyes.

"No, I'm just sad, Laurie. I'm sorry I yelled at you."

"What's the matter, then?" Laurie asked.

"Mr. Taylor told me I can never buy Starlight. It hurts too much to see him when I know he can never be mine."

"Oh, how mean!" Laurie exclaimed. "Well, I'm not going either."

She stayed to help clean the rabbit cages and chicken coop. Miranda worked with a vengeance, putting her anger at Mr. Taylor into her muscles. Laurie did her best to keep up and the chicken coop floor was scraped clean by lunch time. In the afternoon they cleaned out the nesting boxes and lined them with fresh straw. They washed out all the feeders and waterers and scrubbed the roosts.

"What's that?" Laurie asked when Little Brother, who insisted on scampering between their feet, upset a tray of what looked like white scraps of

something.

"Oyster shell. The chickens eat it and it makes their egg shells stronger." Miranda said as she scooped Little brother into her arms and petted him. "You little nuisance. You're no help at all, but you sure are cute."

When the oyster shell was swept out and the tray refilled, Miranda looked at their work with satisfaction.

"That looks so much better. But I feel like all the dirt is on me." Laurie said.

"Me too," said Miranda. "I'm hot and sticky and itchy. Let's ask Grandma if we can go swimming in the pond."

Grandma agreed and the girls set out across the cow pasture. The water was murky, but cool and they splashed and squealed and swam as Little Brother ran around the edge, whining and barking.

"Come on in, Little Brother!" Miranda called.

The puppy lay on his stomach, inching closer, whimpering.

"Oh, all right. I'll help you."

Miranda waded to the shore, scooped him up in her arms and carried him into the deep water. Soon he was swimming after them as they paddled about.

"It looks late, do you know what time it is?" asked Laurie.

"You're right," Miranda said. "We'd better get out. I'm supposed to bring the cows in."

"I don't know if I'm any cleaner," remarked Laurie, "but I sure feel better."

"We'll have to go take a shower to get really clean," said Miranda picking up a towel and wiping her face. "Let's see if you can spend the night. You can put on a pair of my pajamas and we'll wash your clothes and have them dry by morning."

Miranda didn't go back to Shady Hills until Mr. Taylor asked her to come stay with Elliot a week later.

"I have to meet with a buyer in Three Forks," Mr. Taylor said. "I shouldn't be gone long. I'll come pick you up in half an hour."

Miranda agreed with mixed emotion. She was anxious to see Starlight, but afraid that doing so would break her heart.

"I haven't seen you at Shady Hills for awhile. What's been keeping you?" asked Mr. Taylor as she slid into the back seat of his Cadillac.

"Yeah, Miranda," Elliot echoed. "I miss you and so does Starlight. You should have seen what he did to Adam."

"What?" Miranda asked, instantly curious.

"He bucked him right off. Adam said it didn't hurt but I could tell it did. Boy was he mad!" Elliot said with a chuckle.

"I thought he was supposed to be working Roman Candle, not Starlight," Miranda said.

"He has been. But he's spending an hour or two on Starlight in the evening," Mr. Taylor explained. "It's a good thing, too. It looks like Sir Jet is going to require a lot of work."

"I bet Higgins could do it with no trouble," Miranda said, thinking that she could too if they'd only give her the chance.

"Higgins just shakes his head when he watches

Adam with Starlight," Elliot said. "But he won't say anything unless Adam asks him for advice. Adam doesn't ever ask."

Shady Hills looked so good to Miranda that she felt her heart would burst. It had been a long week. She couldn't resist going to see Starlight. Drawn to his stall, she watched for his head to appear over the door to greet her. But the top half of the door was closed and latched.

"Has Adam moved him?" she asked Elliot who trotted beside her.

"No. He's in there. Adam was mad after he got bucked off, so he shut him in. He said he was putting him in solitary confinement to see how he liked that."

"That's stupid and mean!" Miranda shouted as she unlatched the door. "What does he think Starlight could possibly learn from that except to hate Adam more?"

Starlight nickered, and pushed the top half of the door open. He nudged her with his nose.

"He is happy to see me!" Miranda exclaimed. "I was afraid he'd forget me. And I didn't even bring him a treat. I'm sorry, Starlight."

"I bet you could ride him," Elliot said.

"What makes you think that?"

"You've done it before, haven't you?" asked Elliot.

"How'd you know?" Miranda asked with a nervous laugh.

"I saw you, actually," Elliot said. "But don't

worry. I won't tell."

"Is Adam in the bunk house?"

"No. He left."

"How soon will he be back?"

"He drove to Butte to catch a plane for California. He'll be gone at least a week."

"Your Grandfather gave Adam a week off? Was there a funeral or something?" Miranda asked, glad to hear that Adam was gone from Shady Hills.

"No, no funeral. He said he wanted to visit a friend," Elliot told her.

"Must be a good friend. Last I heard, he didn't have enough time to get horses ready for the races Mr. Taylor wants them in."

Miranda stroked Starlight's velvety nose as she talked, her mind racing.

"Grandfather was not happy. He said there was too much to do and Adam said there would always be too much to do. He said the work can either wait or Grandfather can find someone else to do it," Elliot said.

"Well, I'm glad he's gone and I hope your grandfather tells him not to come back. I know I could train Starlight, if your grandfather would just let me."

"He might if you asked him, but he probably thinks you're too little. He'd be afraid you'd get hurt and he'd be responsible."

"I know; that's what grownups always say. Elliot." Miranda turned to him suddenly. "Would you tell if I ride Starlight tonight?"

"No. But are you sure you should when there are no grownups around at all."

"That's the only time I can. Besides, Higgins is in the bunk house. You could go tell him, if anything happened," Miranda said, "not that it will. I won't get hurt, I promise."

"Higgins went to his nephew's house to spend the night," Elliot said quietly, "but go ahead if you want to. I won't tell."

Chapter Eleven

Miranda slipped a halter on Starlight and brushed his coat. He hadn't been brushed out after Adam rode him.

"Hold him for me while I go get the saddle," she said handing the lead rope to Elliot.

When she brought the English saddle into the stall, Starlight shied away almost jerking Elliot off his feet.

"What's wrong, Starlight?" Miranda asked. "You weren't scared of this the last time I showed it to you."

But he seemed to be afraid of it now. He snorted and arched his neck, backing up as Miranda walked toward him.

"What did Adam do to make him hate the saddle?"

"After he got bucked off," Elliot said, "Adam

jerked off the saddle and hit him with it!"

"Easy boy, " Miranda said, lowering the saddle and reaching a hand out to him. "I would never hit you."

Starlight slowly calmed down and nuzzled Miranda's outstretched hand. She patted his face and scratched his neck as she murmured to him. Slowly she raised the buckle of the girth and began scratching him with it. Starlight half closed his eyes as he relaxed. After a few minutes Miranda pressed the saddle against his side as she continued to pet him. He didn't object so she slowly pushed it up onto his back. Scratching him as she reached under him for the strap, she loosely fastened it around him and then gradually tightened it. Starlight tensed and turned his head to look at her, but stood still.

"I'm not going to hurt you, Starlight. I bet Adam cinched it up too tight." Miranda said. Turning to Elliot, she added, "I'm going to lead him up and down the paddock a few times, okay?"

"I'll come with you."

Finally, Miranda led Starlight next to the fence and stopped. She petted him as she climbed the fence rails. When she was about to put her leg over his back, he stepped away with his back feet. Miranda jumped into the saddle before it moved too far away. Starlight reared slightly and then jumped forward. Miranda grasped the pommel with her left hand pulling back on the halter rope.

"Whoa boy. Easy!" she said, patting his neck.

Starlight stopped and turned his head to look back at her quizzically. She had taught him the meaning of "whoa." Through the reward system she had taught him several voice commands and apparently he had learned them well.

"Good boy," she said with a laugh. "Are you looking for a treat for obeying so quickly?"

Leaning forward, she reached down until Starlight turned his head to nuzzle her hand. She patted his soft nose.

"He's looking for sugar. Wish I'd brought some," Miranda said to Elliot.

"If Grandfather knew you were giving him so much sugar, I think he'd be angry. He says it ruins their teeth," Elliot told her.

"You're probably right. Well, I'll make sure to bring him carrots or apples from now on."

Shifting her weight forward slightly, Miranda said, "walk!" and Starlight walked forward. Up and down the paddock they went, first at a walk, then a trot and a gallop. Miranda used only voice commands and the shifting of her body weight to control his speed. She used leg pressure and a slight tug on the halter rope to turn him. When she wanted to stop, she only had to say, "Whoa."

"He's trained, Miranda. He does everything you tell him to do!" exclaimed Elliot in surprise.

"I know. He's the smartest horse in the whole world, isn't he Elliot?"

"He must be," Elliot agreed, "or else you are a

very good teacher."

"It's almost dark!" Miranda suddenly realized. "Have you had supper yet? I'd better get Starlight unsaddled and feed you before Mr. Taylor gets home."

"I am hungry. Grandfather wanted you to warm up something from the freezer for me to eat."

"Oh, I'm sorry, Elliot. You must be starving. I'll hurry. Just remember, don't tell your grandfather what I've been doing."

"I won't, but I think you should. If he knew what you could do, he might let you ride him. Then you wouldn't have to wait until everyone was gone."

"No. I want to surprise him when Starlight's completely trained so he can see that I know what I'm doing. He never said I couldn't ride Starlight, but he might if he thought it was unsafe," Miranda explained as she put the tack away. "The main thing is not to let Adam find out. He expects me to obey him but I don't have to and I won't."

Miranda heard her grandmother talking on the phone the next morning.

"I see," Grandma said. "Well, maybe you're right. As long as there's an adult on the place. They are becoming very accomplished riders, and as long as Miranda wears her helmet any time she rides..."

Miranda watched Grandma hang up the phone, wondering what the adults were planning for her and her friends.

"Mrs. Bergman and Mrs. Langley are both

much too busy to spend a day at the stables watching you kids ride," Grandma explained. "Heaven knows I don't have time. So, we've decided that as long as there is an adult around, you all wear your helmets, and you stay close to the stables, we'll let you stay without us watching over you."

"Hooray!" Miranda shouted, hugging Grandma. "Now we can go everyday?"

"I didn't say that. You'll have to wait until you have a ride both ways, but for this week, at least, you're set. Both Chris's and Laurie's mothers have agreed to take turns bringing you home. You can ride with Grandpa in the mornings, because he's putting up hay on Mr. Taylor's north meadow," Grandma explained. "But, I didn't know if you'd want to. You passed up several chances last week."

"I do," Miranda said. "I missed Starlight and I can tell he missed me, too."

When Grandpa stopped at the hardware store, after picking Laurie up at her house, Miranda ran in to see if Chris was ready.

"Can't go today," he said. "My grandparents are coming to visit, and Mom says I have to help clean the house before they get here. It looks plenty clean to me, but she doesn't think so."

"I'm sorry. Will you go tomorrow?"

"I doubt it. We'll be doing family things. But you can ride Queen, if you want."

"Really? Thanks, Chris." Miranda had the sudden impulse to hug him, but the look of surprised horror on his face as she stepped forward to do so, quickly brought her to her senses. She turned and ran to the truck.

"Let's go for a ride," suggested Laurie, as Miranda came from Starlight's stall. "I got Lady's stall clean and we can clean Queen's when we get back."

The three friends had fallen into the habit of doing chores for each other if one of them happened to be absent. It didn't take long because the horses spent most of their time outside in their paddocks.

"But we can't go to the river pasture without a grownup with us. Anyway, that's what Grandma said," Miranda explained.

"I know. Mom said that, too. But we can ride around the buildings. Let's pretend it's the olden days and we're riding into a new town on our horses. We can explore all the old buildings down by the barn. We might find an empty one we could use for a house."

Riding Queen, Miranda led the way down the lane past the corral to the old barn. Turning right, she rode along a thick hedge of bushes between some old buildings and the field. There was a big open shed with rusty farm machinery in it, and a wooden granary. Miranda could see the back of the tack shed on higher ground behind them. She looked at the back of the hay sheds as Queen moved on. In the distance she could just see the top of Higgins' house. When Miranda looked back at the lane Queen was following, she saw a large oval race track, surrounded by a tall, white board fence. She pulled Queen to a stop and stared in surprise. There was even a metal starting gate that had been pulled out of the way into the center of the oval.

"Laurie, look at this. Let's race," Miranda shouted as she entered the open gate to the track.

They galloped around the track and then stopped.

"Laurie, I have to tell you a secret, but don't tell any of the grownups. It's a surprise."

"What is it?"

"I've been riding Starlight. He's very gentle with me, but he bucked Adam off."

"Really? I'd be scared to get on him. He is so big and he hasn't been trained."

"That's just it. Adam is trying to train him and he's just making him wild. Starlight likes me and I got him to go on the longe line when Adam couldn't."

"Wow! Does anyone else know?"

"Chris knows, and Elliot saw me ride last night when I was baby-sitting."

"You rode when you were baby-sitting? What if something happened to you? What would Elliot do?"

"Laurie! I don't need a lecture! Nothing happened!" Miranda was beginning to wish she hadn't confided in Laurie.

"Sorry, I guess you knew what you were doing," Laurie apologized. "I'd just be worried about how Elliot felt, that's all."

Miranda remembered Elliot's wide eyes and how he'd run to the fence when she had jumped on Starlight's back. He could have been stepped on.

"No, you're right. It wasn't fair to Elliot. I think it scared him," Miranda admitted. "Besides, he must have been starving before I finally got off and got him something to eat. The next time I babysit, I'll spend all my time with Elliot. I'll make sure he gets something to eat and goes to bed on time."

"Well, I didn't mean to preach. I think it's awesome that Starlight lets you ride him. I wish he was all yours and you could tell Adam to leave him alone."

"Me too. I'd love to tell Adam he is spoiling my horse so he'd better stay away from him. That's what he says to me."

"Let's race around the track again," Laurie suggested.

"I'll be right back," said Miranda. "I'll race you on Starlight."

Chapter Twelve

"Wait!" shouted Laurie, turning Lady to follow Queen through the gate.

Miranda urged Queen into a canter as soon as she passed the old buildings. Stopping in front of the tack shed, she swung off and dropped to the ground. She was unfastening the cinch of Chris's western saddle when Lady trotted up the driveway and stopped in front of her.

"Miranda, you'll just get into trouble again. We can have fun on Queen and Lady. We never did play the game I suggested."

"I'll play with you on Starlight. Now's my chance while Adam's away. Oh, wait a minute. You don't think Lady's in heat, do you?"

"How would I know? She doesn't act any different than usual," Laurie said.

Miranda told Laurie about the trouble she and

Chris had with Queen. As soon as the story was out of her mouth, she added, "but don't say anything. Chris and I are the only ones who know."

"Now I'm afraid to let Lady get near Starlight," Laurie said.

"I know. Put Lady in the round pen," suggested Miranda. "I'll bring Starlight over to it and see if he pays any attention to her. If he doesn't, then it's probably safe to bring her out and ride with me."

Starlight showed no interest in the buckskin mare on the other side of the iron bars. Laurie slowly opened the gate and led Lady out. The horses remained calm as the girls led them back to the stable, side by side. Miranda put an English racing saddle on Starlight.

"I've never tried putting a bridle on him. I don't know which one Adam used."

"What did you use before when you rode him," Laurie asked.

"Just the halter. Maybe that's what I'll use this time too."

"You scare me, Miranda. I don't want to see you get thrown or have another runaway."

"Look at this," Miranda called from the tack shed. "Here is a bridle without a bit. I think I'll try it. I don't think Starlight needs a bit in his mouth."

"It looks brand new," Laurie commented.

Miranda put it on Starlight and led him into the paddock. She was just getting on when she heard a car start up. Looking up she saw Mr. Taylor's

Cadillac back out of the garage. She quickly led Starlight back into his stall and out of sight. When the car disappeared over the hill toward the county road, Miranda led Starlight back outside and got on. He responded well to her voice and leg cues. When she wanted to stop him, she pulled back on the reins, putting pressure on the nose band. Starlight backed up.

"This is great, Laurie. Let's take them down to the race track."

Hesitant to push her luck too far, Miranda dismounted and led Starlight through the stable.

"You go ahead with Lady and I'll lead him a little way behind," she said.

Starlight snorted and shied at everything new he saw on the way down to the track. A loose piece of tin on the roof of the old granary flapped in the wind, and Starlight jumped sideways, jerking the reins from Miranda's hand. She fell to her hands and knees, but leapt back up again and held out her hand.

"Easy boy," she said softly. "It's nothing that will hurt you. Come on."

Starlight had already lost interest in the noisy tin and looked ahead at Lady. He whinnied as Miranda took his reins and began leading him again. *I should have put his halter on to lead him down here,* she thought.

Once inside the race track, Starlight stepped forward quickly, his neck arched, and his ears pointed forward.

"Look at him. The race track excites him,"

Miranda called to Laurie. "I bet he's going to love this."

Miranda mounted again by using the fence and lowering herself lightly into the saddle. Starlight flicked an ear backward, as if to say, "I know you're up there." He started at a brisk walk, and she didn't urge him any faster as he caught up with Lady. She kept him to a walk all the way around the track. When she shifted her weight forward and squeezed with her knees, he surged ahead, cantering faster as she continued to lean over his neck.

"Hold on, Starlight," she said, pulling back lightly on the rein.

He shook his head and thrust his nose forward, pulling the reins through Miranda's hands. She grasped them tighter, but didn't pull back any more.

Wondering what he'd do if she just let him have his head, she rested her hand on his neck and bent over it. Starlight shot forward.

She gripped a hand full of his mane with her left hand, swallowed hard, and concentrated on keeping her balance. It wasn't a rough gait, just a very fast one, as Starlight's feet thundered beneath her. Her eyes blurred with tears from the wind in her face. She closed them for a minute. When she opened them, they were flying past Lady and Laurie. They had made a lap around the track. Laurie was holding Lady still and calling to Miranda.

Miranda didn't want to stop, but she thought Laurie looked frightened. She straightened up and shifted her weight to the back of the saddle. Starlight slowed to an easy canter and circled the track once more.

"Whoa, Starlight," she called as she pulled back on the reins.

Starlight came to a jolting stop right in front of Lady. Miranda bounced forward and then regained her seat.

"Wow," Miranda said.

"Wow," Laurie echoed.

"I think he was born for this. He was having fun!" Miranda exclaimed.

"Weren't you scared, going that fast?" asked Laurie.

"Nope. Well, maybe a little at first. But the faster he ran, the more exciting it was. I felt like I was part of him. I loved the feel of the wind."

It was a feeling that stayed with her all evening and brought her happy dreams all night.

When Miranda and Laurie arrived at Shady Hills the next day, Mr. Taylor was leading Roman Candle to the tack shed. He tied him to the hitching post, went inside, and came out with a racing saddle.

"Are you going to ride, Mr. Taylor?" Miranda asked.

"No, I'm too heavy and my knees don't bend like they used to."

"I could ride him for you," Miranda offered.

"I have a jockey coming out. He should be here any minute now," Mr. Taylor said.

"Oh, is he going to ride on the race track?"

"Of course," Mr. Taylor answered. "So you've been snooping around and found the track, have you?"

"We didn't know it was a secret. We just happened to see it when we were riding Queen and Lady yesterday. Is there anything wrong with us riding down there?"

"No. Just stay away from those old buildings. I don't want anybody getting hurt."

A small yellow sports car rumbled over the cattle guard. Miranda watched as it parked near the garage and a small bowlegged man got out.

"Good morning. Mr. Snyder?" Mr. Taylor asked, extending his hand. "This is the gelding we want to take to Great Falls next week. I want you to make sure he's ready. Warm him up before you let him run. These girls can show you where the track is. I'll be down with my stop watch in half an hour."

Laurie was leading Lady out of her stall. Grabbing a bridle from the tack shed, Miranda hurried to get Queen. She saddled her as quickly as she could while the jockey talked with Laurie. Miranda climbed on Queen and led the way to the track.

The girls watched with interest as Snyder rode Roman Candle around the oval, fighting to keep him at a walk. Roman Candle tossed his head and pranced sideways, eager to run. When Snyder finally let him canter, the horse thrust his nose forward, laid his ears back, and lengthened his stride. Snyder tried to check his speed, but the horse took the bit and ran faster. When Mr. Taylor and Elliot got there, Roman Candle was flying around the track, with the jockey bent over his neck, urging him on. Mr. Taylor clicked the stop watch.

"He's fast enough," Mr. Taylor said, "if he can just keep it up."

By the fourth lap, he was starting to slow just a little; not enough to tell by looking, but Mr. Taylor said the stop watch said so.

"He's not running as fast as Starlight did yesterday," Laurie whispered.

"I'd give anything to be able to bring him down and race him against Roman Candle," Miranda whispered back.

"You've got to hold him back the first couple of laps and then let him have it. Save that last burst of energy for the home stretch," Mr. Taylor told Snyder when he finished.

"Yep. That's what we've got to work on. I'll come every morning and again in the evening. We don't have much time if we're going to race him in Great Falls on Sunday."

So much for working Starlight while Adam's gone, thought Miranda.

When Snyder and Mr. Taylor left the track, Elliot asked, "Grandfather, may I get Sunny and ride on the track with Miranda and Laurie?"

"Not today; we're going to a horse sale at the Bridger Stallion Station. We better get going so we don't miss half of it. I want to talk to some buyers."

Miranda and Laurie said good-bye to Elliot and rode Lady and Queen onto the track.

"Let's race. This will be the starting line," Miranda said, lining up Queen even with the power pole near the gate.

Laurie rode up beside her and stopped.

"Ready?" she asked.

"Ready, set, GO!" Miranda shouted.

Queen jumped forward at Miranda's signal. Lady, not to be left behind, ran after her. Queen maintained her lead easily. Continuing around the track for another lap, Miranda leaned forward and shouted into Queen's ear. Queen ran faster. At the end of the third lap, Laurie had stopped and sat on Lady, facing her. Miranda leaned back, pulled on the reins and shouted, "Whoa."

"Wow, Miranda, you're a natural born jockey! I think you had Queen going as fast as Roman Candle," Laurie said.

"It is so much fun to go fast! I wish I could ride in a real race. If I could just ride Starlight, I'd beat any horse in the world."

"Maybe someday you will," Laurie said.

"I don't suppose anyone will let me because I'm too young. And when I grow up, I'll be too big to race. Did you see how little that jockey is? I'll be bigger than that when I'm in high school. My mom is almost six feet tall, and look at my grandpa."

"It's too bad, since you like it so much. I get kind of scared going that fast. Besides, Lady isn't as fast as Queen or Starlight."

"Mr. Taylor's surely gone by now. Let's go get Starlight," Miranda said.

Miranda found that Starlight was as eager to run as Roman Candle had been, but she held him back. It only took a little pressure on the noseband of the bitless bridle to slow him down. When she stopped him at the imaginary starting line, she told Laurie to say go. At the first cue from Miranda, Starlight leapt forward with such power she had to grab his mane to hold herself on. Regaining her balance, she bent over his neck, standing in the stirrups so that no weight was in the saddle. She talked to him all the while he was running, but made no other effort to either slow him or make him run faster. She could not detect any slowing as she rounded the third lap. Wondering if he had anymore than what he was giving her, she shouted to him, "Go, Starlight. Go now!"

He surged forward faster.

It took another two laps around the track to get him slowed down and stopped. Miranda patted his neck and smiled at Laurie. Then she looked up and saw the stooped figure of Higgins silhouetted against the sky on the hill near his house. He was lowering a pair of binoculars.

Chapter Thirteen

Miranda was putting her pajamas on when the phone rang. She heard her grandmother talking in the kitchen as she crawled into bed. She was almost asleep when Grandma came to the door of her room.

"Are you awake, Sweetie? Your mother is on the phone. She has some news for you."

Miranda took the cordless phone from her grandmother and sleepily pressed the talk button, "Hello?"

"Mandy, you hung up on her," Grandma said with a laugh.

"Oh, sorry. I was so sleepy I wasn't thinking, What did she want?"

The phone rang again, and Miranda answered.

"Miranda, are you sitting down?" her mother asked.

"I'm in bed, why?"

"I've got some wonderful news and I don't want you falling over."

"What is it, Mom?" Miranda sat up.

"Adam will be coming back tomorrow, and I wanted to tell you myself before he got there."

"Adam? You've seen Adam?" Miranda shot out of bed and began pacing the floor.

"Sure. Didn't you know he came to California to see me?"

"To see you? Why? I knew he was gone but, why would he take off work like it was some emergency just to go see you?" Miranda couldn't keep her voice from rising as she felt her face grow hot.

"That's what I've called to tell you. He proposed to me. We are getting married!"

Miranda fell to her knees, then sat on the floor, too stunned to keep up the pacing.

Adam arrived at Shady Hills the next day, just in time to load Roman Candle into the trailer for the trip to Great Falls. He smiled at her when she got out of Grandpa's truck.

"Good morning, Miranda," he called cheerfully. "Did you hear the good news?"

"No. I didn't hear any good news!" Miranda said with a scowl, hurrying to Starlight's stall to get out of his sight.

"He was friendly," commented Laurie, following Miranda in and closing the door behind her.

Miranda's mind was spinning and her heart

pounding. She couldn't answer. Seeing Starlight at the far end of his paddock, she decided it was a good time to clean his stall. On her way to get the pitchfork and wheelbarrow she kept her chin up and stared straight ahead, refusing to acknowledge Adam with so much as a glance.

But Adam was busily fighting Roman Candle who didn't want to walk into the trailer.

"What's up, Miranda?" Laurie asked as she returned. "What news was Adam talking about?"

"The worst news in the world!" Miranda snapped.

"Don't yell at me," Laurie said. "I didn't do anything."

"I'm sorry. I didn't mean to yell at you," Miranda said with a sigh. "He asked Mom to marry him, and she said yes."

"Oh, wow! That means Adam is going to be your stepfather!" Laurie exclaimed with a smile.

"It's not something to be happy about!"

"Why not? When they get married, you'll have a regular family like you always wanted. You won't have to live with your grandparents anymore."

"I like living with my grandparents. I'm used to it. I never wished for Adam to be part of the family. I want my dad back."

"Like that's going to happen?"

"I know." Miranda conceded. "According to Adam, Dad's dead. But if Mom wants to get married again, why Adam? He's my worst enemy."

The next day was Friday and Chris came with them to Shady Hills, anxious to ride his horse and be with his friends.

"All we did was go sight-seeing and go out to eat. Do you know how boring it is to sit in the back seat of the van with a bunch of old people?" Chris complained.

"Where did you go?" asked Laurie.

"Yellowstone Park, where the only animals we saw were people in strings of cars going about twenty miles an hour, then the Museum of the Rockies and shopping in Bozeman, and the Mining History Museum in Butte, to name a few. Way too much to try to do in three days."

"Poor Chris," Miranda said with a laugh. "While you were out seeing the world, we were having horse races."

With Adam, Mr. Taylor, and Elliot gone to Great Falls, Miranda felt pretty safe to take Starlight to the track. After a few laps at a walk, trot, and canter, Chris challenged the girls to a race.

"Sure, I'll race you," Miranda said, "if you don't mind getting beat."

"We'll see about that," Chris said. "Are you in, Laurie?"

"No, I'll tell you when to go," Laurie answered.

"Okay, once around the track. Get on your mark!" Chris shouted.

When Laurie yelled GO, Starlight shot off the

line, with Queen only a neck length behind.

"Steady, now," Miranda said, relaxing in the saddle, "We'll let them think they have a chance."

In the backstretch, Miranda leaned farther forward, raising up in the stirrups. Starlight sped ahead.

"All right, now. Go, Starlight. GO!"

With another surge of speed, Starlight seemed to fly across the finish line. He was almost half way around the track again when Miranda started slowing him down. When she came to a stop she saw Higgins standing near the fence with his walker. His nephew, John stood behind him with a huge grin on his face.

"Higgins, what are you doing here?" asked Miranda in alarm.

"I had to see this close up; the fastest horse this ranch has seen since they quit racing Cadillac's Last Knight. Actually, Sir Jet might be faster, you weren't going all out until the last were you?"

"I'm not sure if that was his fastest. I wasn't pushing him," Miranda answered.

"Wait until Cash hears about this!" Higgins said. "He won't believe it until he sees it."

"Oh, no, please. Don't tell him," begged Miranda.

"Are you afraid he'll punish you for riding after he sees what you've done with this horse?"

"I'm afraid he'll never let me ride him again. He'll say he's too good a horse for a little girl. And if he races him and Starlight wins, he will never let me buy him."

"Well, have it your way then," Higgins conceded, "but he will put him in a race whether he knows about this or not. He's already sent in an entry for a race at Yellowstone Downs in Billings at the end of August."

"But how could he? Adam hasn't even managed to stay on him yet," asked Miranda, not wanting to believe this was possible.

"Adam swears Sir Jet will be ready, and from what I've seen just now, he already is."

Miranda spent the night with Laurie and they whispered and giggled after they went to bed and the light's were out. When Laurie was quiet for a few moments, Miranda closed her eyes and dozed off. A loud voice downstairs jolted her back from dreamland. She felt Laurie's body grow tense.

"Laurie?"

"I was hoping you were sleeping," Laurie whispered.

"What's going on?"

"Mom and Dad are arguing. He must have just got in from his trip to Oregon."

"Your parents arguing?" Miranda couldn't believe it. To her the Langleys were the ideal couple, the perfect parents.

"They have been lately, when they think I'm asleep. Mom wants to go back to Cincinnati because of the way every one treats her around here. Dad says there is no sense in letting people control their lives just because they don't like the color of his skin."

"Oh, no. Is it that bad for your mom? What do people do?"

"It's what they don't do that makes it hard. They never talk to her when she goes to the school or the store. Conversation stops when she goes into a room. She asked to join the garden club, and they said they didn't have room for any new members. And then a week later, Mrs. Duffy, the new kindergarten teacher joined."

"That's terrible. Chris's mother is in the garden club. Was she against your mom?"

"I don't think so, but she went along with the others. Anyway she's still in the club with them."

"But your mother is so nice and so much fun. I don't get it." Miranda truly could not understand.

"They think it's a sin or something for a white woman to marry a black man. Mrs. Smythe as much as told her so. She said that God didn't intend for races to intermingle any more than he meant for birds or animals to interbreed."

"That's Stephanie's mother! No wonder those girls were so mean to you if that's the way their parents talk."

"I know. They try to be friendly now, but you can tell they're uncomfortable. One time I saw Tammy in the store and I said, 'Hi'. She started to wave until she saw her mom was watching and then she just turned her back and walked away."

"Laurie, what if your Mom gets her way and you move back to Cincinnati? I couldn't stand it if you had to leave. You are the best friend I ever had." Miranda was frightened by the idea and clung to Laurie's hand.

"I know. I don't want to go. I love it here with you and the horses. Chris is a good friend too, and I don't care about the others."

There was no more sound from downstairs and Miranda thought Laurie's parents must have gone to sleep. She tried to imagine what it must be like to be all grown up and not be able to feel welcome. Miranda thought it was only something that happened to kids.

A phone rang loudly in the hallway.

"Who in the world would be calling this late?" Laurie asked, jumping out of bed and running to answer.

But it quit ringing before she got there. The girls listened as a door opened and closed downstairs. They heard voices.

"Let's go see what's up," Miranda suggested.

Laurie nodded and they hurried downstairs.

"Don't tell me you girls are still awake!" Mrs. Langley said.

"We heard the phone. Who called?" Laurie asked.

"It was Miranda's grandmother. She's the only one who'd let us know," Laurie's mother answered. "There's a fire at the Smythe's place. The fire trucks are so far away, they're asking volunteers to come help put it out. Preston insists on going, even though they'll probably send him back."

"Lives could be at stake, not to mention the loss of everything they own. Let's don't let some stupid bigotry make us forget what's important here," Preston said as he went out the door.

"Back to bed, you two," Mrs. Langley said.

"But Mom, we couldn't possibly go back to sleep now," Laurie said.

"Well, me either," Mrs. Langley sighed. "Let's get in the car and see if there is anything we can do."

"Thanks, Mom," Laurie said.

They slipped into their shoes, pulled jackets over their pajamas, and went out the door. As they neared Smythe's ranch house, they saw flames.

Cars lined the road and people were milling about. It was the barn that was on fire. Miranda saw Stephanie standing in a thin nightgown, staring at the flames and shivering.

"There's a blanket in the back seat. Let's get it," Mrs. Langley said.

"Here, Stephanie," Laurie said, wrapping it around her classmate.

Stephanie didn't seem to notice.

"Steph?" Miranda said.

"My horse. Dad said he probably got out, but I don't see him," Steph said.

"Look, someone's going in there," Laurie shouted.

"That's Billy! Someone stop him!" Stephanie

cried.

Miranda had seen Preston Langley walking toward them, but when Laurie shouted, he turned and sprinted toward the barn.

"Don't go in there!" yelled a firefighter who had just arrived on the scene. "Stop that man."

Two or three men ran to intercept Mr. Langley.

"No, Dad," Stepanie screamed, as the three girls watched a man grab Mr. Langley's arm.

Mr. Langley punched the man with his free arm and pulled away, jumping into the back door where they had seen little Billy Smythe disappear.

Timbers were falling in the front part of the barn and the fire was rapidly spreading along the roof toward the back. Mrs. Langley and Laurie held each other tightly as they stared in horror at the burning barn.

A shout went out as a horse, then another ran from the burning barn. In the midst of the horses, five in all, a man staggered out carrying a child. Miranda watched Mr. Smythe run toward the man, then stop a few feet from him. He stepped back a step or two and then fell to his knees as he held out his arms.

The barn collapsed in a shower of sparks as Mr. Langley stumbled, and Mr. Smythe clutched his child tightly.

Chapter Fourteen

Miranda found herself flying across the barnyard, her hand still clutching Laurie's. Mrs. Langley sped passed them and threw her arms around her husband just as the girls reached him.

"Are you all right?" Mrs. Langley sobbed. "I've never been so frightened in my life! You could have been killed!"

"Get to a phone and call 911," Mr. Langley ordered. "The boy is unconscious."

Mr. Smythe was rocking back and forth, sobbing. Mr. Langley put his hand on the man's shoulder and shook him.

"My wife's getting an ambulance, but the boy may need CPR. Do you know how?"

Smythe looked wildly, into Mr. Langley's face which was blackened by smoke until only the whites of his eyes shown out of the darkness. He didn't seem to comprehend and just clutched his boy tighter.

"Hurry, he's going to die if we don't start now," Mr. Langley said, pulling the boy from his father's strong grip.

Mr. Smythe pushed Mr. Langley away, but his wife and daughter grabbed his arms.

"Let the man help!" Mrs. Smythe cried. "We can't let Billy die!"

Mr. Langley lay Billy on the ground and tilted his chin up, felt his neck for a pulse, and checked for breathing.

"Heart's still beating but he's not breathing," he said as he leaned down and covered the boy's mouth and nose with his own mouth and forced air into the child's lungs. He repeated this procedure, counting slowly between breaths. He stopped again to make sure there was still a pulse.

Not until a few minutes before the ambulance pulled in, did Billy cough and began to cry. His mother, who had been kneeling beside them, took him into her arms and rocked him gently until two paramedics came. They finally had to pry Billy from his mother's arms so they could put an oxygen mask on him and lay him on a stretcher.

"What about you, sir?" asked one of the attendants. "Your jeans are soaked with blood, we'd better have a look at your leg."

Miranda looked at Preston Langley. He was sitting on the ground now, holding his thigh, pressing his forehead against his knee.

"Get this man into the ambulance, too. He's lost a lot of blood," the paramedic said.

Mr. Langley didn't protest as they put him on a stretcher and loaded him in the ambulance along side Billy. Mr. Smythe started to climb into the ambulance.

"Let me ride with my son. He needs me," Mr. Smythe begged as an attendant blocked his way.

"Sorry. You'll have to come in your own car. We're taking him to Bozeman Deaconess. You can meet us there."

"Come on, girls," Mrs. Langley said to Laurie and Miranda. "We're going to Bozeman."

They arrived just after the ambulance and hurried to the emergency room. Miranda saw Billy on a stretcher. He was sitting up, talking to his parents.

"Billy, are you okay?" Miranda called to him.

"My throat hurts," he said, "but I'm all right. Did the horses get out of the barn?"

"Yes. I counted five as they ran out."

"Good. That's what Dad said, but I thought maybe he was just trying to make me feel better."

Miranda turned to follow Laurie and Mrs. Langley who were still looking for Mr. Langley.

"Wait, Miranda," Billy called. "Who got me out of the barn? I don't remember anything but black smoke and falling down. Dad just said it was some man."

"Well, I guess it was some man!" Miranda ex-

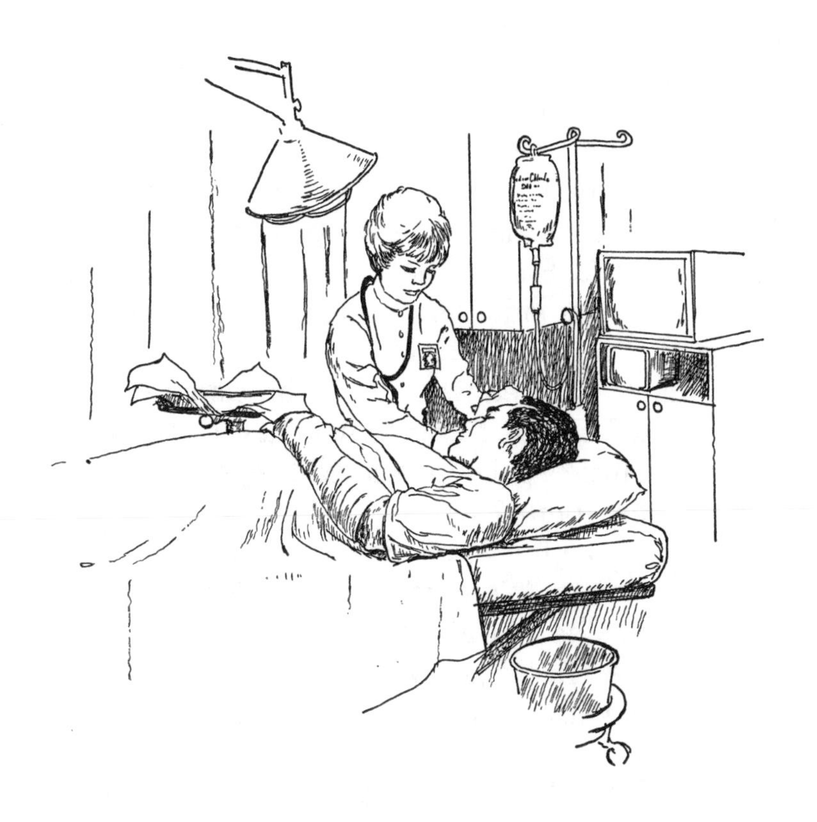

claimed indignantly. "It was Laurie's dad, the only one brave enough to run into the fire. He saved your life."

After a nurse washed the smoke from his face, Mr. Langley looked pale yellow, in spite of his dark skin. A doctor examined the deep cut on his leg.

"This is going to take a lot of stitches," the slender young doctor said, "but first I want to get some blood back into you. We've got to get some airlifted from Billings unless you have a donor."

"Let me give you some of my blood. We'll know it's safe," Mrs. Langley said.

"If you're sure, Honey."

But Mrs. Langley's blood type didn't match. Laurie insisted on having hers typed. It was the same as her father's. She was taken into another cubicle, Miranda by her side. Mrs. Langley stayed with her husband.

Laurie winced when the technician inserted a needle into her arm. Miranda held her friend's hand noticing Laurie's pale lips and wide eyes.

"Does it hurt?"

"Only a little when they first put it in," Laurie insisted bravely. "Nothing like Dad's leg must hurt. Do you think he'll be all right?"

"Sure. The Doctor will sew him up, they'll give him your blood, and everything will be fine," Miranda answered.

"Okay, all done," the technician said. "You lie here while I take this to your father. I'll bring you something to eat and drink. Don't get up until I get back."

When the technician was gone, Laurie started to sit up, but quickly lay back on the pillow.

"Wow, I'm dizzy."

"Really? You look awfully pale," Miranda said. "You'd better wait until you get something to eat."

"Stephanie's Dad didn't seem very grateful, did you think?" asked Laurie, changing the subject.

"No. Did you see him try to stop your dad when he was running to the barn. He acted like he wanted to throw him off his place."

"He's a jerk. But at least Billy's safe. My dad could have been killed. I hope they realize that."

A nurse brought Laurie a glass of grape juice and a granola bar.

"Rest awhile after you finish this," she said.

When the girls finally went back to Laurie's father, they saw Mr. Smythe standing in the hallway, twisting his cap in his hands and looking nervously toward the cubicle where the curtain was drawn around Mr. Langley.

"Uh, would you tell your dad thanks. I guess he saved my son's life," Mr. Smythe said to Laurie.

"Why don't you tell him," Laurie asked. "I think it's the least you could do."

"Yeah. I just didn't know if I could go in there."

Miranda held the curtain back and said, "Sure you can."

"Uh, Mr. Langley. I don't deserve what you did today for my son. I want to say thanks." Mr. Smythe was looking at the floor.

"I didn't run into that barn because I thought you deserved anything. I ran in there because a life was in danger. Everyone deserves to live, especially your boy. But I'd have done the same if it had been you trapped in there."

"Really?" Mr. Smythe looked up in surprise and then moved slowly to Mr. Langley's side.

Letting go of his tortured cap, he held out his hand to Mr. Langley. This time he looked him in the eye before he said, "Thanks. Thank you from the bottom of my heart."

Mr. Langley gripped Smythe's hand firmly and nodded.

"Your leg," Mr. Smythe asked. "How bad is it?"

"It'll be fine. I'll be on antibiotics for awhile, but the doctor expects it to heal with no problem. I must have ripped it on a nail, so they gave me a tetanus shot, too."

"I'll be glad to pay for your doctor bill and anything else I can help you with," Smythe offered.

"Not necessary. I have insurance that will take care of it."

"What about the deductible? I'll pay that."

"No, but thanks. If you really want to show your appreciation, just put in a good word for me with the school board the next time they get ready to hire a teacher."

Mr. Smythe blushed and looked at the floor again. He nodded and then met Mr. Langley's gaze.

"Okay. I'll do that. You can count on it."

When Miranda returned to Shady Hills the next day, Elliot ran to meet her with news about how well Roman Candle had done in Great Falls.

"He was in three races and he won them all," Elliot said. "Grandpa told Adam to start working Sir Jet — well, you know he means Starlight — every day so he can win in Billings. He said that if Starlight runs like Roman Candle did, it'll put Shady Hills on the map and everyone will be bringing their mares to have them bred to a winner."

Miranda tried to hide her disappointment. She wished she hadn't taken Starlight to the track. Teaching him to race was like giving him away. If Mr. Taylor had his way, she'd never be able to call Starlight her own.

Adam began immediately. He didn't try to longe him anymore, but put him on the exercise wheel every morning before starting his workout. He put a light harness on him and began driving him from the ground. Miranda watched from the sidelines with a sinking heart.

"He's a smart horse. He's catching on to this reining in no time," Adam said to Mr. Taylor when he came to the arena to watch.

"When are you going to get on him? The race is just five weeks away. I don't even know if he'll run."

"What will you do if he doesn't?" Miranda asked hopefully.

"What are you doing here?" Mr. Taylor asked, seeing her for the first time. "I thought you were off playing with Chris and Laurie."

"You know how much I care about Starlight. I have to watch. What if he won't run?"

"I've got another horse ready, a half sister to Starlight, I mean Sir Jet. Her name is Fancy Cadillac. That doesn't help me prepare a horse to take Knight's place, though. How about it, Adam? You going to ride him today?"

"Yeah, I guess so," Adam grunted, "toward the end of the day when he's not so frisky. You haven't been feeding him, have you, Miranda? He doesn't need any hot feed while I'm training him."

Miranda glared at Adam but didn't answer. She hadn't spoken to him since he got back from Great Falls, and she didn't intend to.

"Nothing but hay for now," Mr. Taylor said.

As much as it hurt Miranda to watch Adam work with Starlight, she couldn't stay away when he saddled him and led him to the round pen. Adam pulled Starlight's head around until his neck was completely bent and his nose touched the saddle. Holding him in this uncomfortable position, Adam put his foot in the stirrup.

"What are you doing?" Miranda asked, breaking her silence. "You're hurting him."

Starlight sidestepped away from Adam. Adam jerked on the rein, tucking the stallion's head until he fell on his side in the soft dirt.

"You idiot!" Miranda screamed running to Starlight's side. "You don't have to hurt him."

Adam grabbed her arm and jerked her back. "You get out of here this minute," Adam shouted, shaking her with both hands. "I won't have you interfering with my work."

Starlight stood up and shook himself violently. When Adam gave Miranda a shove that sent her sprawling in the dirt, Starlight squealed and nipped Adam's arm.

"I hate you, Adam Barber!" Miranda yelled. "Just wait until Mr. Taylor hears what you did."

"Just get out of here," Adam said, rubbing his arm. "I'll talk to Mr. Taylor. You've spoiled this horse so much that I can't do a thing with him when you're around."

Miranda strode off toward the barn, too angry to speak. If she tried, she'd cry and she wouldn't give Adam that satisfaction. She looked back before rounding the corner of the stables. She saw Adam swing into the saddle. Starlight arched his back put his nose to the ground and jumped. Adam sailed through the air and landed on the ground with a thud. Starlight walked to the far side of the pen and stood quietly.

Chapter Fifteen

Elliot's voice reached her. He was calling from the barn door.

"Miranda are you in here?"

"Up here, Elliot," she answered from the hay loft. "Come on up if you want."

"No! You come down!" he shouted. "Grandfather just took Adam to the clinic. He thinks he broke his arm, and he told me to stay with you until he gets back. They just left Starlight standing in the pen with his saddle half way off."

Miranda was down the ladder before Elliot could say more. They ran to the round pen together. Starlight nickered a greeting and walked to the gate as they opened it.

"Are you all right?" Miranda asked, patting his nose.

"Adam told Grandfather that Starlight bit

him," Elliot said.

"He did. I saw it. And Adam deserved it," Miranda assured him.

She led Starlight to the fence so she could reach the billet straps which were now on his back because the saddle hung low on one side. It fell to the ground when she unfastened it. She put it away and brought out a brush and her favorite red halter. Taking off the bridle, she snorted at the strange looking bit. It had very long shanks, and the mouthpiece was hinged at the sides and had a high and sharp curb in the middle. The chain that went behind his lower lip was very loose, allowing the middle part to dig into Starlight's palate at the slightest pressure on the reins.

"This is cruel! I ought to throw it away. Starlight doesn't need it. The way Adam was jerking and pulling on it, I wouldn't be surprised if Starlight's mouth is bleeding," Miranda exclaimed. "I wish your grandfather would fire Adam. He may be a good riding instructor, but he's a terrible horse trainer."

"Maybe he won't need to fire him if Adam has a broken arm," said Elliot.

"That's right! Now maybe Mr. Taylor will give up on racing Starlight and take Fancy to Billings instead."

"He's taking her and Roman Candle too. He plans to race all three." Elliot said. "All he has to do is find another jockey. Mr. Snyder is already signed up to ride for someone else."

Miranda fell silent. It hurt to think of someone

else riding Starlight to victory.

"Where are Chris and Laurie?" she asked.

"They're riding down at the race track. Shall we go watch them?"

"Sure, I think I'll lead Starlight, just to give him some exercise," Miranda said.

"Don't you want to ride him?" Elliot asked, as if he'd read her mind.

"Sure I do, but I decided I wouldn't do that anymore when I'm supposed to be taking care of you. I'm sorry I did it last time."

"I don't mind. I'm not a baby."

"I know but... maybe if Laurie wants to stay with you while I ride... you know, so you have someone to talk to," Miranda said.

"If Grandfather wasn't so worried about me riding without a grownup around, I'd get Sunny and ride, too," Elliot said.

"I know. It isn't really fair."

"You don't mind his rules, so maybe it would be all right if I didn't, either" Elliot suggested.

"No, it wouldn't. If anything happened to you, it would be my fault." Miranda was horrified at the example she was setting. "Besides, I'm not breaking your grandfather's rules. It was Adam who said I couldn't ride Starlight, and I don't have to mind him!"

"But you don't want Grandfather to know."

"No, but I figure if he lets me feed him and exercise him, he probably knows that I'd be riding him too," Miranda clung to this reasoning and hated having to question it.

"Anyway, I'm not going to ride Starlight now," Miranda said with sudden decision.

"Is that because of me, or are you afraid Grandfather will come home and see you?" Elliot asked.

"You're too smart, Elliot. I guess it's both," Miranda admitted.

Elliot seemed bent on keeping her honest.

Miranda had a message to call her mother when she got home.

"Is there a problem between you and Adam?" her mother asked as soon as she said hello.

"What do you mean?" Miranda asked.

"Adam called and said he broke his arm. I asked how and he said something about a horse that you insist on spoiling. I asked him to explain and he wouldn't. What was he talking about?" Mom asked.

"He broke his arm because he got bucked off of Starlight. That's his own fault."

"Were you there when it happened?"

"Yeah, I was watching. I couldn't believe he'd twist Starlight's neck to get on him. I think he's afraid of Starlight!" Miranda exclaimed.

"Listen, Sweetie," Mom said. "You don't know everything there is to know about horses. How could you? You're only eleven. Adam has been working with horses for years. Why don't you just stay away if you think he's being too rough?"

"Is that what you'd do if someone was being too rough with me?" Miranda asked hotly.

"No! Why? Is anyone hurting you, Miranda?"

"No, not really," she answered, not wanting to be a tattletale. Besides, Adam's little shaking hadn't hurt her all that much. Just her pride. "I'm just saying I love Starlight, so I can't just let people hurt him without trying to stop it."

"Do you have any idea how much it hurts me

to have the two people I love the most fighting with each other?"

"I don't know; maybe as much as it hurts me to have people mistreating the horse I love."

When Miranda arrived at Shady Hills the next day, Adam came out of the bunk house with his arm in a sling. She glanced at him and headed quickly to Starlight's stall.

"Hey, Miranda, wait." Adam called. "I want to talk to you."

Miranda stopped and slowly turned around, frowning. She wasn't interested in listening to another lecture from Adam Barber. She wished he would leave her alone.

"I talked to your mother last night. Well, I do every night," Adam said with a nervous laugh.

Oh, that's nice, thought Miranda. *She calls me once a week if I'm lucky.*

"She's worried that I don't like you. I told her I do. I think you're a great kid. I just wanted to be sure you know that."

Miranda didn't answer because all the things she wanted to say would be far too rude.

"Well," Adam said, "how about it? You don't think I hate you do you? I know you used to think that, but I thought we had that all straightened out when I told you about your father."

"May I go now?" Miranda asked.

"Not until you answer my question," Adam

said. His smile disappeared quickly.

"I don't know if you hate me," Miranda answered. "I just know you act like it."

"I do not!" Adam shouted. "Just because I don't always agree with you, doesn't mean I don't like you. You'll figure that out some day."

When he turned and walked away, his sharp voice echoed in Miranda's ears. She walked slowly back to Starlight's stable. She should probably try to get along with Adam for her mother's sake, but she couldn't pretend something she didn't feel.

Miranda didn't dare try to ride Starlight with Adam hanging around all day. She never knew when or where he was going to show up. Instead, she begged Mr. Taylor to let Elliot ride his horse.

"I'll ride with him so he won't fall off," Miranda promised.

"How do I know you won't both fall off?" Mr. Taylor asked.

"Mr. Taylor, you know I'm a good rider. We'll stay close to the house and buildings."

Mr. Taylor agreed. Both Laurie and Chris saddled their horses, and Miranda rode behind Elliot on Sunny. They played hide and seek on horseback until they got tired of that. They played Pony Express and follow the leader. As Miranda and Elliot led the others back toward the riding arena, a FedEx truck was leaving. Adam stood in front of the bunkhouse pulling a letter out of a large red and white envelope. Miranda watched as he unfolded it. His face turned white. He frowned and slowly crushed the letter in his fist. Seemingly unaware of anything around him, he stood like a statue, staring into space.

Adam was gone when Miranda came back to Shady Hills two days later. There was a stranger in the round pen with Starlight. Alarmed, Miranda hurried to the pen.

"Who are you?" Miranda asked.

"Name's Buck Brannaman," the man replied. "What's yours?"

"I'm Miranda Stevens. That's Starlight."

"Starlight? Don't tell me I got the wrong horse. Mr. Taylor told me to work with Sir Jet Propelled Cadillac."

"That's what he calls him. Actually, it's his registered name, but I call him Starlight," Miranda said. "I want to buy him."

"Oh, I see," Buck said with a smile. "Does Mr. Taylor want to sell him?"

"Not if he wins the races he is going to have him run in."

"In that case, I don't suppose you want him to win."

"No," Miranda admitted, "and he wouldn't if Adam was training him. Adam doesn't understand Starlight."

"What can you tell me about Starlight?" Buck asked. "Do you think he can run?"

"Maybe," Miranda answered cautiously. "He

was injured, you know."

"Yes, I've seen his scars. He seems pretty sound, though. How well do you know this horse?"

"I know him better than anyone. He loves me." Miranda said.

"Then I bet you could be a big help to me. Would you like to give me some pointers?"

Miranda couldn't believe her ears, but she was suspicious.

"You're the only grownup that thinks I know anything," she said. "But why would I help you? I want to buy him, but if he wins, Mr. Taylor is going to keep him to replace his Thoroughbred stallion."

"Well, then, I'll just have to figure it out for myself, I guess. I'd like to help you, but if he's a winner, I can't help that. I have to do the best I can. Not just because I'm paid to, but because I owe it to Starlight to give him my best, as I do every horse I work with."

Miranda watched Buck. He was in no hurry, it seemed, but he was already gaining Starlight's confidence in ways that Adam never had. Miranda had believed that Starlight was a one person horse; that he would perform for no one but her. Buck Brannaman just might prove this theory false.

Chapter Sixteen

The phone rang as Miranda and her grandparents were finishing their noon meal the next day.

"Mr. Taylor wants to know if you can come over and stay with Elliot this afternoon," Grandma said, cupping the receiver in her hand. "Do you want to?"

"Sure," Miranda said, jumping up from the table.

"I'll take you over there. Mr. Taylor has to leave right now, but Elliot will stay with Higgins until you get there."

When Miranda arrived, she knocked on the bunk house door and Elliot opened it quickly.

"I'm in the middle of a game of checkers," he said. "Do you mind if I finish before we go?"

"Of course not," Miranda said. "We can stay as long as you want. Hi, Higgins."

"Come on in, child. You haven't been to visit me since Adam moved in. Make yourself at home," Higgins said. "Maybe you can play the winner."

"Sure, if that's okay with Elliot, I'd love to stay and play."

She watched them play for a moment and then wandered around the room. It was much more crowded now that Adam had moved in. There was a desk by the window and a large leather recliner crowded in beside Higgins' easy chair. There were pictures of pickup trucks with pretty girls in swimming suits hanging on the wall where Higgins used to have a painting of a cabin near a mountain stream. Adam's desk was neat and tidy, but the waste paper basket was overflowing beside his desk.

"I'll take the trash out for you while you finish the game," Miranda offered, picking up the waste basket and stuffing a crumpled piece of paper from the floor into it.

"Thanks, that would be great. The one under the sink is full, too," Higgins said. "There are trash bags under there. Just bag it all up and set it on the back porch. I'll have John haul it to the dumpster tomorrow when he comes."

Miranda stopped putting papers in the bag when she saw the word "certified" stamped on a crumpled letter. She smoothed it out and read:

> Dear Mr. Barber:
> We regret to inform you that your wife,

> Geraldine Elizabeth Barber, was killed in a boating accident last Wednesday. Your daughter, Margot, is being held by the Sedgewick County Department of Health and Welfare, Wichita, Kansas, in a foster care facility until you can come for her or make other arrangements. Please call...

Miranda folded the letter and put it into her pocket. Her heart was beating rapidly. *Wait until Mom hears about this,* she thought. *When she finds out the secrets Adam has been keeping from her, she'll call off their engagement for sure.*

She couldn't keep her mind on checkers and Higgins beat her in about three minutes. Elliot wanted to challenge her to a game, but she suggested they go outside and play for awhile.

"Elliot, I know a secret about Adam," Miranda said when they were in the loft of the old barn.

"What?" Elliot asked.

"Adam has a daughter! That's why he left."

"Really? How do you know?

Miranda pulled the letter from her pocket and read it to Elliot.

"Wow. Will he bring her here? How old is she?" Elliot asked eagerly.

"I don't know. The letter doesn't tell. I wonder what Adam will do?"

"I hope he brings her here," Elliot said.

"Why? You don't know her. She might be a brat or a baby or have something wrong with her."

"I don't care. She's a person isn't she? It would be fun to have another kid living here."

"Well, don't get your hopes up. Your grandfather might fire Adam and hire the new guy that's working with Starlight."

"Oh, Mr. Brannaman doesn't want the job. Grandfather just hired him for this one time."

"He really knows what he's doing. I'm afraid I'll never get to buy Starlight, now. I watched Mr. Brannaman riding him, and Starlight didn't buck at all. Starlight likes him."

As soon as Miranda got home that evening, she went to the phone.

"Grandma, may I call Mom?"

"Yes, in fact she called you today and I told her I'd have you call back."

Her mother answered on the second ring.

"Mom, I have some news for you!" Miranda said.

"All right. I have some for you, too. You go first."

"Adam isn't as wonderful as you think he is. He has a wife and kid that he never told you about."

"Oh, really?" her mother said, with a laugh. "And just how did you find that out?"

"It's true and I can prove it!" Miranda was exasperated at her mother's amused tone.

"I believe you. In fact that's what I called to tell you. I just met Margot, and I think you will love her. She is quite a cutie."

"You met Adam's daughter? Adam is there?" Miranda dropped into a chair.

"Yes, he's here. He arrived this morning. Is something wrong, Miranda?" Mom asked.

"I can't believe you don't care that he was married and had a baby that he never told you about."

"That's where you're wrong. He told me all about them before he asked me to marry him. I told him I wanted to meet his daughter and that I wished he could get full custody so that she could live with us after we get married," Mom said. Miranda was speechless, so her mother went on. "I'm sorry his ex-wife died. Margot is terribly sad, of course, but I will do everything I can to be a good mother to her, and you will have a sister. Isn't that something you always wanted?"

Later, when Miranda was lying in bed in the dark, and the whole conversation kept repeating itself in her mind, she couldn't remember how she answered that question. She only remembered thinking, *how about being a good mother to me?* She lay awake for what seemed like hours. When at last she fell asleep, she had a bad dream. When she awoke, it was much later than usual. As she remembered the events of the past week, she just wanted to fall asleep again. Her Mom was going to marry Adam in spite of how Miranda felt. Some kid named Margot was taking her place in her mother's life — a place Miranda wanted, but never had — at least not for a long, long time.

Miranda went into the bathroom and locked the door. Looking into the mirror, she complained to her reflexion. It was a habit she'd almost forgotten.

"Adam's trying to take Dad's place, and I won't let him," she began, looking into the stormy gray-green eyes.

"But you never even knew your dad," the reflection reminded her.

"But Mom did and she loved him. He was brave. Adam would never give his life to save someone else!"

There was no answer and Miranda slid to the floor, covered her face and sobbed. She felt abandoned by the mirror child who used to comfort her. At times like these, Miranda often turned to dreams of her horse for consolation. That was when she still hoped that he would someday belong to her. Now with Buck Brannaman training him, he'd surely win every race. He'd become famous and Mr. Taylor would never part with him. Everyone would call him Sir Jet, and they'd never know about the little girl who had saved him and won his heart. Miranda went back to bed and cried herself to sleep.

Adam hadn't returned by race day. Since he was unable to work with a broken arm, he decided to stay in California and spend time with his daughter.

"That way, she can get to know me and I can help Adam help her get over the heartache of losing her mother," Mom had explained to Miranda on the phone.

Miranda heard about all the fun things they were doing together. Her mother was a nanny for Kort, a toddler who was the son of a rich fashion model in Los Angeles. Together, Mom and Adam were taking Margot and Kort to the beach, to Disneyland, and Sea World. Miranda was sick of hearing about how much fun they were having. But Mom always reminded her, "You know you can come live with me anytime, Miranda. There is room for you here, and as you know, Kort's mother said it would be fine."

If Starlight won this race in Billings, her chances of ever having him for her own would be doomed. It would be torture to see him win. But, it would also be hard to see another horse beat him, because she believed he was the fastest horse in the world. It was hard to know what she wanted anymore. She wanted to be with her friends and her grandparents and Starlight, but she wanted to be with her mother, too. She didn't want to be around Adam or share her Mom with two other kids. She was so mixed up, she couldn't even decide if she wanted to go with Mr. Taylor to Billings to watch the race after her grandma said she could.

When she arrived with Grandma at Shady Hills, Buck was loading Starlight into the horse trailer. She couldn't help liking Buck, even though he was helping to take her horse from her.

"Are you going to ride him in the race?"

Miranda asked him.

"No, I've got other work to do, I'm heading for a ranch up by Kalispell to help turn some mustangs into cow horses."

"When will you be back?"

"I doubt I will. I'm not normally a race horse trainer. Mr. Taylor called me as a last resort. I enjoyed it though. You've got quite a horse there."

"Me? He belongs to Mr. Taylor. And I don't

think he'll ever be mine." Tears welled up in Miranda's eyes.

"There's more than one way to own an animal," Buck said. "People who think of a horse as a piece of property are content to own the title to him as long as he makes the owner some money. But people who see a horse as a free spirit, like you and I do, know that a horse really belongs to no one except to the one he gives his heart. For Starlight, that's you."

Chapter Seventeen

Miranda put her arms around Buck's waist and hugged him. She couldn't hold back her tears even though it embarrassed her for anyone to see her cry. Buck patted her back as she cried.

"I wish you could be my dad," Miranda said. "If my mother could meet you, I know she'd like you better than Adam and marry you instead.

Buck took her by the shoulders and pulled her away, squatting down to look her in the eyes.

"I really like you, Miranda, and I'd love to be a part of your life. But, I'm afraid that wasn't meant to be. I have a wife and family who I just couldn't trade for any other. You have to take the family you have and make the most of it."

"Will I ever see you again?" Miranda asked, ignoring the tears that streamed down her cheeks.

"I don't know, but whether we do or not, we'll

always be friends, right?"

Miranda nodded and wiped her tears away.

"Miranda! You're going with us! Yippee." Elliot shouted from behind her.

Until that moment she'd been unsure if she would go. But, with Elliot's encouragement, she realized she couldn't bear to be left out of Starlight's big moment. Even if he wasn't her horse, Buck Brannaman had said she owned his heart. She wouldn't let him down or leave him until she had to.

We're going to be all the way past Billings if he doesn't turn off soon, thought Miranda as she watched for some sign of a race track. At last she saw a billboard that said "Yellowstone Downs next exit." As she looked ahead, she could see the huge grandstand at the race track to her left. It looked like there were a lot of people already there. She peered out the window as they left I-90 and drove toward the Metra Center. She wished Mr. Taylor would drive faster. She had been disappointed to learn that they wouldn't be riding in the truck that pulled the horse trailer. It had gone a full hour before Mr. Taylor got ready and backed his Cadillac out of the garage.

"Mr. Taylor!" Miranda exclaimed as he drove past a driveway where a sign said, Yellowstone Downs, Horse Unloading Here. "You missed the gate. There are the stables and all the horse trailers!"

"No, we park over there. That entrance is just for people bringing horses in."

"But we have horses there. Shouldn't we go see about them?"

"I hired a groom and a driver to take care of them. I'll go over there later, but first I'll get us situated in the box I reserved, right above the finish line. Then I need to talk to some people before the race."

After Mr. Taylor gave his name, they were allowed through a turnstile into the area under the stands. Mr. Taylor picked up a racing schedule before leading the way through an array of tables where people sat eating, drinking, and filling out forms. Miranda saw the track and ran to the fence.

"Up here," Mr. Taylor said, going up the stairs and into the stands.

He walked into a wooden box with chairs in it and was greeted by a white haired man in a gray suit. Mr. Taylor shook his hand and they began talking, ignoring Miranda and Elliot.

"Look," Elliot said. "They're bringing some horses onto the track."

Horses with jockeys in various colored silks perched on tiny racing saddles were led by horses with riders in western saddles and blue jeans.

A voice crackled over the loudspeaker, announcing the first race and that it was ten minutes to post time.

"Where's Starlight?" Miranda asked, trying to see around the tall man in front of her.

Mr. Taylor didn't hear her at first. She waited for him to quit talking with his friend, tugged his sleeve and asked again.

"I don't see Starlight, or any of our horses," she said.

"Oh, he doesn't run yet. We don't have a horse in this race. Roman Candle is in the next one."

"Who's riding Starlight? Who's taking care of him? Shouldn't we go to his stable until it's time for his race?"

"You're sure full of questions," Mr. Taylor complained. "The answer is no. We can see the races from here."

"But..." Miranda began.

"Hello, Harry," Mr. Taylor turned away from Miranda to shake hands with a bald-headed man in a white suit.

"You never answered all my questions!" Miranda muttered, knowing he wouldn't hear her above the noise.

Miranda held Elliot's hand and looked around in wonder at the track below. Riders were heading for the starting gates.

"Number seven is in," said the voice over the loudspeaker. "Now number five, number two and number six are loaded. It looks like there is some difficulty with number three."

Miranda strained to see the starting gate far down the track. She could just make out a very dark bay, tossing his head. He kicked and reared as the rider applied his whip to the horse's hips. The rider stayed on as two men led him back behind the gate and out of sight. Miranda strained to hear the announcer.

"Iron Side's Cannon is refusing to enter gate number three...allow five more minutes. If his handlers can't get him in, we'll have to start without him." the loud speaker crackled.

Would they actually start a race without one of the horses? Miranda hoped with all her heart that Starlight would refuse to go in when it was his turn. If he didn't race he couldn't win, and maybe Mr. Taylor would give up on him.

The bay was led to the front of the gate. Miranda thought he was beautiful with his black tail and close cropped mane. He had a blazed face and two white socks, one on the right hind foot and the other left front. She hoped he wouldn't give in. It would serve his rider right for whipping him. But after a little coaxing, the bay backed into the starting gate.

Soon a bugle sounded and the race was announced. The gates opened and twelve horses sprung forward. Miranda watched them fly around the track, trying to find Iron Side's Cannon among the pack.

"Go, Cannon, Go!" Miranda shouted.

"I can't see," Elliot said, tugging on Miranda's arm.

"Stand in the seat. I can barely see, myself."

"Who are you shouting for?" Elliot asked.

"There he is, he's in third place now. See the bay with the white face?"

She watched in excitement, barely able to contain herself, as Ironside's Cannon passed another horse and was gaining on the leader. In the final stretch, with a sudden burst of speed, the leader pulled away. In a moment the race was over, and Cannon had dropped to fourth. Miranda sat down in a wave of disappointment.

"It's just a race," she lectured herself, knowing no one would hear her. "You don't even know that horse. Wait 'til Starlight runs."

It seemed like an eternity before the next group of race horses was led onto the track to file past the crowd. Roman Candle was ridden by a short but broad jockey, one of the best, according to Mr. Taylor.

Roman Candle's race was so close, they had to wait for the results of a photo finish to find out whether he or a filly named Misty Lane had come in first. Finally the announcer called out Roman Candle's name. Mr. Taylor grinned broadly, slapped her on the back and squeezed Elliot's shoulders.

"That's a great start for Shady Hills," he said, "Now if Sir Jet runs like I know he can, we'll see another victory."

"Is Starlight next?" Miranda asked anxiously.

"No, he's in the 10th race," Mr. Taylor said. "You two wait right here. I'll be right back."

It was a long time before Mr. Taylor actually returned. The third race began and ended long before he came back.

"Mr. Taylor, let's go see Starlight while we're waiting for his race. It's going to be a long time,"

Miranda suggested as soon as she saw him.

"I just did. I had to talk to the jockey — congratulate him, and make sure the one who's supposed to ride Sir Jet is ready."

"You went without us?" Miranda asked.

"Yes, I was in a hurry. You'll see him soon enough when he races."

Miranda fumed silently. Mr. Taylor knew how much she wanted to be with Starlight, yet he went without her. Had Adam convinced him that she caused Starlight to act up when she was around? It just wasn't true and it wasn't fair to keep her away from her horse.

Fancy raced in the fifth race. She was behind at first, pulling into third place in the back stretch and then gaining in the home stretch to pass the second, then the first horse and win by a nose.

Mr. Taylor went wild again, laughing and shaking hands with everyone around him before telling Miranda and Elliot to stay right there. He'd be back in a minute.

"Yeah, I've heard that before," Miranda said to Elliot.

But this time he was back before the next race started. Elliot curled up on his chair and put his head on Mr. Taylor's shoulder. He was soon sound asleep. With no one to talk to, Miranda was soon bored. The time between races seemed to be getting longer. She looked at Mr. Taylor who was busy talking to his buddies about which horses to bet on in the next race.

"I'm going to the restroom," she said. Mr. Taylor glanced at her and went on talking.

When she came out of the women's room, she stood for a moment between the grandstand and the track, which was fenced off with tall woven wire. She looked back at Mr. Taylor who was studying his racing schedule and writing something down. She'd be back before he could possibly worry about her. She turned left and ran along the fence in the direction of the starting gate. Soon the woven wire fence ended and a lower fence separated her from the track. Straight ahead sandstone cliffs towered about fifty feet above the level of the track. Beneath them was a road that circled behind the race track.

She followed it toward the stables. There were many buildings and she had no idea which one Starlight was in, so she went to each one, peering into each stall. She saw three exercise wheels with a couple horses on each one. When she had looked in every barn, she gave up and started back toward the track. Then she saw him. He was saddled, a rider was on his back, and he was being led around the track by a man on a gray mare. They must have gone out while she was in or behind one of the stables.

Miranda ran to get back to Mr. Taylor before the race started. But she was too late. Before she got back to the starting gate, she heard the announcer say they were loading the horses in the starting gate. She hadn't seen Starlight's number so she didn't know if he was in or not. But there was nothing said about any trouble getting the horses in the gates.

"They're off. Number 6, Sir Jet Propelled Cadillac is in the lead by a length. What a surge of speed out of the gate. His rider is pulling him in, saving him for the home stretch. This horse is a newcomer, but his owner, Cash Taylor has high hopes for this one. We can see why. He's fighting the bit. Good Lord, he's bucking. Red Cyclone runs into him. Cyclone's rider is on the ground. Red Cyclone is out of the race as he runs to the inside rail and stops. With the rest of the pack half way down the track, Sir Jet is

spinning in circles. It appears his rider is fighting for control."

Miranda strained to see, but a very tall metal fence around the back stretch stood in her way. She ran to it and peered through the narrow slits between the wide curved rails. She could just get the toes of her boots between them and began climbing.

"The gray filly, Dew Cross, is taking the lead on the inside. Wolfgang's Malady is a close second. What's this? Sir Jet is closing in on the pack. He's catching them, passing on the outside. In the back stretch, he's in third place. Wolfgang's Malady is putting on a burst of speed and is ahead by a nose, a neck. Sir Jet is coming up on the right, almost neck and neck with Malady. Sir Jet's rider brings out the whip. Sir Jet is stopping! He's fighting the rider. Look at that horse buck!"

Chapter Eighteen

The horses had thundered past Miranda just before she reached the top of the fence. As she looked over the top, she saw the rider bring down his crop on Starlight's rump. Starlight shied, skidded to a stop, and began bucking and twisting. The other horses streamed past him as his rider flew over his neck and rolled on the ground. Climbing over the fence, Miranda jumped to the track and ran to the stallion.

"Starlight. Come here, boy. Easy."

The rider was up and running to the fence as Starlight wheeled and ran toward him and Miranda.

"Wolfgang's Malady wins by a length, Dew Cross is second and...Good Heavens! Sir Jet has dumped his rider and is chasing him off the track. I've never seen anything like it, folks. What's this? A child is out there with him. This looks like a killer horse, folks and there is a little girl on the track!"

The rider was trying to climb the tall fence, as

he shouted at Miranda.

"Get away from that horse, you fool!"

"Starlight, it's okay, boy," Miranda crooned as walked toward him with her hand extended.

He trotted toward her, ears pricked forward and nuzzled her shirt pocket. Miranda pulled a bag of carrot sticks from her jeans pocket and fed him. As she lead him toward the gate, she saw several men rushing toward her. Starlight stopped.

"The girl is leading the stallion as if...Wait. Those men are scaring him. Watch out little girl."

Miranda patted Starlight on the cheek and talked softly to him.

"Stay back," she called as the men approached. "I'll bring him to his stable."

One man strode toward her, and Starlight laid his ears back.

"You're going to make him mad. I'll bring him!" Miranda insisted.

The man stopped.

"I'll follow you," Miranda said.

The man slowly turned and walked away as Miranda followed with Starlight. Before they had gone far, Mr. Taylor emerged from the crowd.

"Miranda Stevens, what on earth are you doing down here?" he shouted. "We'd have won the race if you weren't in the way. Adam was right about you. Now give me that horse!"

"I didn't do anything!" Miranda exclaimed. "Starlight didn't even see me until after he threw his rider. He bucked because the jockey hit him!"

"You have no business down here," Mr. Taylor shouted, reaching for the rein.

Miranda placed it in Mr. Taylor's hand as she blinked back tears. Starlight nickered to her as Mr. Taylor led him forward.

"Elliot's up in our box with Harry. Go back and stay there until I get back."

As Miranda trudged back to the grandstand, a man with a microphone stopped her. A camera man stood behind him with a huge camera aimed at her.

"Excuse me, Miss. What's your name?"

"Miranda Stevens."

"That was an extremely brave thing you just did out there. Weren't you afraid?"

"What brave thing? All I did was go get my horse."

"That horse was attacking his rider and yet you..." began the reporter.

"He was not!" Miranda interrupted. "Starlight was running to me because I called him. He always does that."

"Starlight? Don't you mean Sir Jet?"

"That's what Mr. Taylor calls him, but I call him Starlight and that's the name he answers to."

"I'm confused. It says in the race book that Sir Jet Propelled Cadillac belongs to Cassius Taylor, yet you call this horse Starlight and claim he is yours."

"Mr. Taylor owns him on paper, but Starlight's heart belongs to me. He's a free spirit and he loves me," Miranda said, repeating Buck Brannaman's words.

"Well, evidently what's on paper carries more weight because I just saw Mr. Taylor walk off with a black horse that I assume is both Sir Jet and Starlight. Am I right?"

Miranda nodded and tears filled her eyes, "I want to buy him, and I thought Mr. Taylor was going

to let me when he was hurt, but when he got better..."

"When Mr. Taylor was hurt?"

"No. Starlight. Mr. Taylor didn't want him when he was crippled. But now..." Miranda stopped, embarrassed.

"But now," prompted the reporter.

"Mr. Taylor wants to keep him," Miranda said.

"Why do you think he threw his rider when he was so close to winning the race?" asked the reporter.

"Because his rider was beating him. He doesn't need a whip to make him run. He's not used to it."

"How do you know what he's used to? Have you ridden him?"

"Yes."

"At a run?"

"Sure."

"As fast as he was running today, before he tossed his rider?"

"Faster," Miranda said.

Miranda felt a fim hand grasp her by the arm and pull her away from the reporter. She looked up into Mr. Taylor's angry face.

The ride home was long and silent. Miranda sulked and Mr. Taylor steamed. Elliot slept in the seat against Miranda's shoulder. The three horses rode in the back of the long trailer, behind the ranch truck, driven by a new man that Mr. Taylor had hired to take Adam's place temporarily.

When Mr. Taylor let Miranda out in front of her house, he didn't say a word and neither did she. Elliot murmured a sleepy good-bye and Miranda squeezed his hand. Grandma was sitting at the table doing paper work when Miranda came in.

"Hi, Sweetie. How was it?"

"Terrible," Miranda answered.

"Do you want to talk about it?"

Miranda nodded and Grandma led her to the couch and put her arm around her shoulder.

"Did Starlight win his race?"

"No, but he would have if I'd been riding him. His rider whipped him. It was the jockey's fault he lost, but Mr. Taylor is blaming me."

"Blaming you?" asked Grandma. "How could that be?"

Miranda told the whole story, including the interview.

Grandma shook her head as Miranda finished.

"Mr. Taylor is right about one thing. You should not have gone off without his permission, and you definitely shouldn't be on the race track. Miranda, when will you learn to stay out of trouble?"

"But it didn't hurt anything. It's a good thing I was there. I bet those other guys couldn't have caught him. Everyone else was half afraid of Starlight. He would never hurt me, Grandma."

"I know you believe that. The fact remains, you put your life in danger. Mr. Taylor has every right to be angry with you," Grandma said.

"He's not mad about that. He's mad because Starlight didn't win and that's not my fault."

"I'm sure he's angry about your disobedience, and rightly so," Grandma said. Looking at her watch she added, "Let's see if you made the ten o'clock news."

Sure enough, there was a clip of the race. It focused on Starlight from where the jockey raised his crop to where Miranda handed him over to Mr. Taylor. There was even a portion of the interview which ended with the reporter saying, "Will Starlight, perhaps the fastest horse this track has seen in a long, long time, ever win a race? According to Miranda Stevens, he would if she rode him."

"That's not what I said," Miranda argued. "It's true, but I wouldn't say it on television."

"You said plenty on television," Grandma reminded her. And suddenly Miranda realized just how much she had revealed that she hadn't wanted anyone to know.

Miranda didn't return to Shady Hills until Mr. Taylor called two days later to ask her to come stay with Elliot for a couple of hours. Grandma dropped her off and she knocked hesitantly at the door. Elliot let her in.

Mr. Taylor plopped a newspaper down on the table as she came into the kitchen.

"Look at this, young lady. You made a big impression at the race the other day," Mr. Taylor said, pointing to a picture of her leading Starlight.

It was on the front of the sport's section and took up the top half of the page. Miranda stared in disbelief.

"Starlight! They didn't even get his name right, thanks to you," Mr. Taylor went on. "And I saw you on Channel 7 the other night. You made me look like a money grubbing ogre."

"Oh, I didn't mean to, Mr. Taylor," Miranda said as she felt her face turn red. "I didn't know it was going to get on TV and in the newspapers."

"How could you not know? The man had a microphone in your face. Didn't you see the cameras?"

"Yes, but I didn't think..." her voice trailed off.

Miranda felt as if she could cry. She'd been angry at Mr. Taylor, and she hadn't thought of the consequences. Mr. Taylor had taken her to the race. He had let her spend all the time she wanted to with the horse she loved. And look what she had done in return. She wished she could take it all back.

"I really didn't mean to make you look bad and I'm awfully sorry."

"Well, forget it. I'll get over it and so will they. I've got to go."

"Mr. Taylor, It wasn't my fault that Starlight didn't win. He hadn't even seen me when he started bucking. It's because..." Miranda began.

"I know, I saw it on television."

Chapter Nineteen

Miranda went back to Shady Hills with Chris and Laurie on Monday, anxious to spend as much time as possible with Starlight before school started on Wednesday. Elliot ran to meet them.

"I'm getting ready to go with Grandfather and Adam to look at the fillies in the hill pasture. We get to go in the jeep, wanna come?"

"Adam is back?"

"Yes, he got here last night."

"Is his little girl with him?"

"No. He's all by himself," Elliot said. "Come with us, please."

"No, thanks. I'll see you when you get back."

Miranda wondered what Adam had done with his daughter. *Probably left her with Mom,* she thought. *Mom can take care of other people's kids but she doesn't have time for me.* Remembering that it was her choice to be here instead of with her mother, Miranda dismissed those thoughts. She hurried to Starlight's stall. When the jeep disappeared around the corner of the arena, Miranda went to Queen's stall.

"Hey, Chris. Are you going to take Queen to the race track?"

"Yeah, do you want to ride double?"

"No, I want to ride Starlight."

"Are you sure it's safe?"

"You and Laurie put your mares in the round pen and I'll bring Starlight over to see if he's going to act up around them," Miranda instructed.

The horses were all quite calm and soon the three friends were riding to the race track.

"Let's pretend this is a real race," Miranda suggested. "I know how they do it now. But we have to hurry before Mr. Taylor comes back."

"Please don't run so fast," Laurie said. "I don't think it's good for Lady; she's twenty years old. But I can't hold her back when the other horses are running away from her."

"You don't have to race if you don't want to. It can be between Chris and me," Miranda said.

"Okay. You and Chris go ahead. I'll do my own pretend race, only I'll keep her from running all out."

"Say go, then," Chris called.

Starlight began to run as soon as Miranda gave him the signal. When he saw Queen nosing ahead of him, he surged forward even faster and soon left her in the dust. Miranda lay low along his neck, her heart pounding. What a rush! She was on the edge of fear but happier and more excited than she'd ever been.

When they came to the starting line, Starlight made no indication that he was ready to stop and Miranda didn't ask him to. When they came around a second time, she saw that Chris had joined Laurie at the fence. With her friends watching, she leaned farther forward, resting her hands on his neck.

"Go, Starlight! Go, go, go!"

He stretched his already long strides and pushed harder. A thrill of fear passed through her body, but only for a moment.

"Yippeeee!" she yelled when she felt sure of her balance again.

As she flew past Laurie and Chris again, she realized that they were not alone.

"Whoa, boy, that's enough." she said to Starlight as she sat back in the saddle.

He immediately slowed his pace. By the time they came around again he was trotting. Miranda put the slightest bit of pressure on his nose band by pulling back on the reins of the bitless bridle. He stopped. Turning around she walked him back to the fence where Mr. Taylor, Adam, and Elliot stood, staring.

"I told you to leave that horse alone," Adam shouted. "Mr. Taylor ought to have your hide for messing with his..."

"Quiet, Adam," Mr. Taylor interrupted. "I've never seen a horse run that fast before, not even Last Knight when he was in his prime. How did you do it, young lady?"

"I didn't do it. Starlight did. I just rode him."

"That's what I mean. How did you ride him? I've had a number of grown men try without much success. Buck Brannaman was the only one who could handle him and he never got that kind of speed out of him."

Miranda didn't answer.

"Well, you'd better walk him out. He's got to be hot after that," Mr. Taylor said, although Starlight was barely sweating. "Come see me in the house after you put him up."

Adam waited. When Mr. Taylor was out of earshot he said, "Miranda, I feel responsible for you. After all, I'm going to be your stepfather in a few months. Your mother would be devastated if anything happened to you. I'm asking you not to get on that horse again. He is far too much horse for a child."

"You aren't the boss of me, Adam, and marrying my mother won't make you my boss. I'll stay with my grandparents forever rather than live with you," Miranda said as tears of anger stung her eyes. "Why don't you take care of your own little girl and leave me alone?"

"Don't worry about Margot. She's in good hands, and I do take care of her. Let me put Starlight away for you so you can go see Mr. Taylor."

As Adam reached for the reins, Miranda turned Starlight away and trotted him down the track. When she looked back, Adam was walking away.

After brushing Starlight's coat until it gleamed and making sure his water was fresh, Miranda went to the main house.

"Mr. Taylor," she blurted out before he could say a word. "I know what you're going to say, and it isn't fair. I love Starlight and he loves me. I know it was my fault he got hurt, but he got better because of me, too. I don't want any other horse. I just want Starlight. It wouldn't be fair for you to make me stay away from him. If you won't ever let me buy him, please just let me keep taking care of him and riding him sometimes."

Tears were streaming down her face.

"Hold on a minute. You seem to think you know just what people are thinking. Well, you don't. It's Adam who says that you spoil him, not me. On the contrary, I think you've done more for that horse than anyone else. Maybe if he hadn't gotten hurt, he'd be so high strung, no one could handle him on the track. He performs for you because you have won his trust."

"So I can still ride him?" Miranda asked, not daring to believe her ears.

"Yes, in fact, I was thinking we might work out a partnership, if you're interested," Mr. Taylor said.

"A partnership? What do you mean?"

"I have a young man coming next month to ride Starlight for me. He's new at the jockey business so he won't be too set in his ways. If you will teach him how to work with Sir Jet... Oh, all right — with

Starlight — I think we can win some races."

"If he wins, you'll never let me buy him. That's why I never wanted you to see how fast he could run," Miranda moaned.

"I'm not finished yet," Mr. Taylor said, holding up his hand. "If you'll help me with this, I'll sign over half interest in Starlight to you. I'll put your name on his papers as half owner, and I'll make out a contract that says that when I die, my half interest goes to you. In the meantime, you can keep taking care of Starlight as well as working with the new jockey."

"Really, Mr. Taylor?"

"Yes, really. Of course I'll still have the say about when and where he races and how he's cared for. I'll get the money he earns in stud fees and race winnings, until you're eighteen, or I die, whichever comes first."

"I don't care about the money. I just want to know he can't be taken away from me," Miranda said.

"If you promise to work with the new jockey and help make a winner out of that horse you love so much, I'll have the papers drawn up tomorrow. You'll get a copy, so you won't have to take my word for it."

Miranda's head was swimming. What did this mean to her? Would she be selling out if she agreed? She didn't like the thought of someone else taking her place on Starlight, riding him to victory. If only she could race him, but she knew her grandparents would never agree. Besides, she suspected the racing commission didn't allow little girls to ride.

"Well, do you want this horse or not?" Mr. Taylor asked. "I've talked to your grandparents about it and they said it was up to you."

"Yes," Miranda exclaimed. "I'll do it!"

When Adam heard of the arrangement, he was outraged.

"What in the world is the old man thinking!" he shouted. "Giving you permission to go on feeding and spoiling that horse is bad enough, but to put you in charge of his training is preposterous!"

"Did you really tell Mr. Taylor it was all right if I work with Starlight?" Miranda asked her grandparents that night.

"Yes, we were amazed when Mr. Taylor promised to make you a partner. Starlight will become all yours when Mr. Taylor dies," Grandpa said. "I'd love to buy Starlight for you because I know how much he means to you, but that was not an option. Mr. Taylor has plans for that horse."

"But," Grandma said, "you must never ride him without your helmet or race with other horses."

"Not even Queen and Lady?"

"It's especially dangerous around a mare," Grandpa said. "Now if he was gelded it would be different, but Mr. Taylor wants him for a stud. If I'd known you were even thinking of riding him, I'd have warned you about riding him around your friends' mares. You have no idea what trouble you could get into. You've been pretty lucky."

Miranda didn't argue. No sense worrying them now.

"I'll be careful," she said.

Two weeks later, Mr. Taylor found her in Starlight's paddock and handed her an envelope from the thoroughbred registry. Unfolding the papers inside, Miranda saw her name listed after Mr. Taylor's as joint owner of Sir Jet Propelled Cadillac. Then Mr. Taylor handed her another paper: a legal contract, signed and notarized. It read:

"In the event that Cassius L. Taylor wishes to relinquish ownership of his interest in Starlight, or in the event of his death, his interest will revert to Miranda Stevens for one dollar, and she shall hold all rights and title to Sir Jet Propelled Cadillac, otherwise known as Starlight."

Miranda clutched the papers to her chest.

"Thank you, Mr. Taylor." As tears clouded her eyes, she embraced him. "I guess we're partners now, aren't we?"

"I guess we are. Are you happy about that?"

"Oh, Mr. Taylor, all I've ever wanted since the first time I saw Starlight, was to have him for my own.Now I know he can never be taken away from me."

Remembering Mr. Brannaman's words, she smiled. Starlight — heart, soul, and body — was hers for life.

If you enjoyed ***Miranda and Starlight***, ***Starlight's Courage,*** and ***Starlight, Star Bright***, we'd love to hear from you as we plan the rest of the series. ***Starlight's Shooting Star*** is the tentative title for the fourth book of the series. You'll want to read this exciting continuation of the saga of Miranda and her beloved horse, Starlight. It will be available for advance sales by late summer, 2003

For your convenience, we've provided an order form on the back of this page.

Happy Reading and Riding to You!

Raven Publishing
P.O. Box 2885
Norris, MT 59745
USA

To order directly from the publisher,
send check or money order to:

Raven Publishing

P.O. Box 2885
Norris, MT 59745

For more information, e-mail:
info@ravenpublishing.net
Phone: *406-685-3545*
Fax: *406-685-3599*
See us on the web
www.ravenpublishing.net

$9.00 (U.S.) per book plus $2.00 shipping and handling for one and $.50 for each additional book.

Name____

Address____

City____________________________State_____Zip______

Please send me:

_____copies of **Miranda and Starlight**

_____copies of **Starlight's Courage**

_____copies of **Starlight, Star Bright**

_____copies of **Starlight's Shooting Star** (Advance orders after July, 2003)